"Charm is deceptive, and beauty is fleeting, but a woman

who fears The Lord is to be praised…"

Proverbs 31:30

To God's lovely daughters

My sisters in The Lord

Do not give up

Love is real

God will restore

Mysterious Ways

J.T.Hephzibah

Chapter One

There was no way in the world Nikki was going to stand by and let this woman try to squeeze her way in front of her in line. Nikki had been standing in line for almost ten minutes just to buy her boneless chicken breast and fresh herbs for her big date with Joshua. She had managed to get off work early which was nothing less than miraculous given the fact that Sweet Blessings Daycare Center was experiencing an unusually high enrollment for summer camp.
Nikki had been working at Sweet Blessings for five years and she had never seen so many kids sign up for summer day camp.

Erin, the new director had drawn people from all over to the spring open house and it seemed they all had decided to bring their kids to summer camp at Sweet Blessings. Erin was a woman who got down to business and didn't much care whether those who worked for or with her liked her or not. She often said she had enough friends but not enough money. Nikki actually did like Erin although she hated to hear her say she needed more money than friends.

Nikki and Erin had been talking about Joshua for almost a month. Joshua was the new director of the daycare center Erin had run for years before coming to Sweet Blessings. According to Erin Joshua was a widower who had been trying hard to find a woman who didn't think it was odd for a man to work in a daycare center. When Erin first mentioned him to Nikki, Nikki thought Erin had a secret crush on him but Erin soon dispelled that rumor when she revealed to the staff that she going to marry her girlfriend of seven years.

~   ~   ~   ~   ~   ~   ~

When Erin made that announcement most of the staff members who had been quite friendly with her became cold. It was funny for Nikki to watch them all trying so hard to shun Erin while Erin cared so little about their approval that she didn't notice. But Erin did notice how kind Nikki was to her and one day she asked her, "Nikki, why are you so nice? I don't get the feeling you want any favors but there has to be some reason you are so nice."

Nikki smiled at her and answered, "I have no choice. I have to love you." The discussion moved into a ministerial session where Nikki shared her testimony of how she had been involved in drugs and had been an accessory to an attempted murder and how The Lord had pulled her out of that situation and redeemed her. Erin was puzzled, "Your criminal background check came back clean. Attempted murder is a felony."

"Yeah," Nikki admitted, "I know. I should have gone to jail. I should be in jail right now. The night it all happened I drove the car. I didn't know that they planned to kill anyone but I did know they were going to rough him up. He had stolen $250,000 of drugs and thought he was going to get away with it. If I hadn't stayed out in the car on the phone with my homies who were waiting for me to bring back drugs I would have been right there in the middle of it all. But God is good Erin. I couldn't get those fools off the phone for anything! I know some church folks would not agree but The Lord used my addict friends that night to keep me out of that motel room. I had no idea what happened until weeks later when the police showed up at my house questioning me.

Erin was suspicious, "Still Nikki, some thing should be on your record if you were at all connected to it."

"Tell me about it!" Nikki rejoiced, "That's why I am saying what I am saying about God. He does miracles...for real! I did go to jail and when I was there I had nothing to do but pray and the more I prayed the better I felt. I cried and prayed constantly. I had no idea how I had gone from a nice college girl studying early childhood education to a coke whore. One minute I was hanging out with friends having fun drinking socially and smoking weed in college, and the next I was doing lines at clubs after parties. Some where along the lines I became a total addict and was one of the most popular coke whores in Miami. Everybody wanted some of me and if they had money or good drugs they had me."

Erin was intrigued by the story, which was cut off as their lunch break ended. They left the park and went back into the building. They continued the story the following day and from then on the two spent their afternoons together talking and becoming close friends. But their developing friendship did not go unnoticed. There were rumors about them floating around the daycare. Once, Erin's girlfriend, Lisa, had come to the daycare center to confront Nikki. Lisa had not gotten the sensational response she had hoped for.

By the time she left she was looking forward to getting to know Nikki. Any woman who could maintain her cool despite the curses and threats Lisa had thrown had to be strong. Lisa liked strong women. And if there was anything Lisa could pick up on it was sexual energy and as hard as she tried to find it dancing between Erin and Nikki it was not there. She ended up apologizing to Nikki and inviting her over for dinner. Nikki never went over for dinner but the three had gone places together and had become good friends.

~   ~   ~   ~   ~   ~   ~

Standing in the line at the grocery store Nikki realized that she was supposed to be defending her place in line but instead she was daydreaming. The young woman who had stepped in front of her was having trouble with her credit card. Nikki noticed photos of two small children on her key chain and asked, "Are they your kids?"

The girl was not particularly friendly and snapped, "What?"

Nikki asked again, "On your key chain, are they yours?"

The woman smiled, "Oh yeah, my babies. Twins, a boy and a girl." She handed the key chain to Nikki. The two were adorable and looked just alike and yet the masculinity of the little boy and the feminity of the little girl was striking.

Nikki smiled handing it back, "They are beautiful!"

"Yeah, they eat a lot too! All these snacks are about to break the bank!" She began sifting through the bags and removing items. First out were baby carrots, then graham crackers, and she was about to remove some thing else when the Holy Spirit nudged Nikki.

Nikki thought, "Aw come on Lord, she already bullied her way in front of me, now I have to buy her groceries?" It occurred to her that she had not actually been bullied. In fact it was possible that the young woman had not noticed her standing slightly aside from the line and skimming over gossip magazines. And it didn't make her case for being bullied any stronger that she had gone from skimming gossip mags to daydreaming as this woman had made her way to the counter. Nikki thought, "That's what I get for being interested in that celebrity gossip anyway." She took a deep breath and said, "Will you allow me to buy your groceries?"

The woman didn't process what she had said and absently responded, "Huh? Oh yeah, I know it's a lot of little stuff right? My kids are snackers." She pulled string cheese out of one of the bags. "We do have cheese at home."

Nikki said loudly, "Miss, will you allow me to buy your groceries? I don't mean to intrude but I noticed your card was declined and I know how that feels. I mean, I don't have kids but I have maxed out a card or two in my day."

The woman shook her head and frowned, "Oh no, you don't even know me! I've got it. I just forgot that I bought some personal items at Savemart before I came in here. I just have to take about $20 off that's it. No big deal. But thank you."

Nikki noticed the woman did not show any sign of embarrassment and was impressed. She would have left it at that but The Holy Spirit nudged her again. "Oh fine!" she thought. Then she resigned and obeyed the little voice inside her. "Well here, at least take this." Nikki handed the young woman the twenty dollar bill that was in her hand, "That way you can keep the string cheese. I work in a daycare center. I know how kids feel about their string cheese!"

"Oh, no really, I couldn't accept that from you. You don't even know me. That's kind but..." Nikki cut her off.

"Listen, every good and perfect gift comes from The Father above. Take the twenty please. It's not from me. It's from God. He'll pay me back and then some. And trust me, I need all the blessings I can get these days."

The woman looked into Nikki's eyes for a moment. There was no pretense there and no shame. Both women smiled and Nikki handed the $20 to the cashier who was also smiling.

The mother of the adorable twins smiled graciously, "Oh thank you. Little Bobby and Robbi will be glad. It's hard to break it to a three year old that you don't have string cheese but that you have spaghetti!" The women laughed. Nikki had to ask, "Which one is Bobby and which one is Robbie?"

"My son is Bobby, His name is Robert after their dad, my daughter is also named after their dad. Her name is Roberta. We call her Robbi."

Nikki thought that was cute and clever. She smiled nodding, "Gotcha. Well get on home to those little cutie pies."

As the cashier ran the card a last time for $20 less and it was approved, Nikki was relieved but did notice the woman seemed quite stress free. Nikki was more stressed and embarrassed for woman that she seemed to be.

Stuffing the receipt into one of her bags of snacks the woman replied, "I will, and thank you."

"Thank The Lord. He is the One who told me to bless you."

"Well, thank you Lord! Always up to some thing! By the way, did you say you work in a daycare center?"

"Yeah. Sweet Blessings."

"Oh wow! I just enrolled the twins in your summer camp program!"

Nikki was happy to hear that. She wanted to know the little twins Bobby and Robbi whose round faces smiled so brightly on the key chain photo. "Great! So I guess I'll see you around. My name is Nikki. I'll be the head teacher in their age group. Actually there are two of us for the summer but I am going to make sure I get them. What's your last name?"

"Johnson. I am Evelyn Johnson. The twins are

Hudgins though, after their dad. We are together but never got married. We've been together for five years now."

"Well, I'll look for you next week when camp starts."

"Will do. And thank you for the string cheese and whatnot!"

"Anytime." Nikki was feeling pretty good and thanked The Lord for His involvement. She really would have been upset not to have the twins in her class. They were so cute and she liked Evelyn. She paid for her items with her credit card and had a short conversation with the cashier about how good it feels to be in the right place at the right time. Then she gathered her bags and headed home. It was 4:30 and Joshua, Erin and Lisa were due at her house at 7:30. She had plenty of time to straighten up, take a nap and prepare the meal she had planned.

Chapter Two

Benita had been waiting outside Nikki's house for ten minutes when she pulled up. She knew Nikki had forgotten all about their shoe sale date. In all the years they had been friends Benita had never known Nikki to forget a shoe shopping date but some thing about the way Nikki had paused on the phone when Benita mentioned it the night before told Benita that she had forgotten and would forget again when it came time to meet at the mall. Benita decided to wait at Nikki's house instead so they would not have to drive both cars and so she didn't end up waiting forever at the mall and end up buying a bunch of random stuff out of boredom.

Benita saw Nikki's cute little red car pull into the cul-de-sac and got out of her own cute little red car. People tended to assume they had gotten similar cars on purpose but Benita had purchased hers months before Nikki's cousin died and left his to Nikki. It was bittersweet for Nikki to drive the car as she had been in it so often with her silly cousin Matthew. That was over a year ago and still some times Nikki got a little sad when she got in and out of the car with no tall thin cousin Matthew, in the passenger side to complain about her driving. Nikki smiled thinking of how absurd it was that Matthew had always insisted that she drive when they were together and yet he complained constantly about her inability to do so in a lawful or safe manner.

Benita called to Nikki, "Girl, what in the world is wrong with you? Never have I known you to forget about a Shoe Fetish clearance sale! You know Shoe Fetish has probably been packed all day and you are fooling around! Benita noticed the bags in Nikki's hand. "Groceries? You stopped to get groceries when there are shoes at stake? You could have grabbed some thing at the mall woman...after shoe shopping!"

Nikki put her hand on her forehead. Benita knew this to be Nikki's exasperated move so she asked, "Okay, what's the deal? You got off work early so we could go and now you have the tired face."

"Ni, I forgot all about Fetish today."

"Oh my goodness! I reminded you last night! And you got off early for it right?"

"That's not why I got off early."

"Oh, well excuse me. That was our plan wasn't it? I did a 7-3 for this and you know how I feel about day shift."

"I know." Nikki thought for a moment. She knew she could still make dinner in time if she went with Benita but she would not get to take a nap or do much straightening. She knew the adrenaline of the shoe experience would eliminate the need for a nap (especially combined with the nervousness of meeting Joshua) but there was a layer of dust on every household decorative item she owned that needed to be addressed before anyone came over for dinner. "Ni," Nikki whined, "I need a favor." She paused briefly before continuing,

"When we get back will you help me dust a little? I have guests coming over and you know it's a dusty mess in there." The two women walked towards Nikki's townhouse.

"People coming over? Who?"

"Some friends from work."

"Friends from work? What friends from work? Not that lesbian. Oh Lord, you said guests plural...both of them? Girl are you crazy? Anything might happen? Why are they coming here?"

"Ni. Get a grip. What do you think they are going to do to me? It's really not cool how you are about people sometimes."

"How I am about people?"

They entered Nikki's townhouse and Benita plopped down in her favorite spot, the Papasan chair in the corner as she chider her friend, "All I know is you better not let anybody sit in my chair and leave any perverse spirits in it!"

"Ni!"

"What? For real, you are supposed to be sanctified...set apart. The Bible says the wicked have no place amongst the righteous."

"The Bible says love your neighbor as yourself."

"The Bible says..."

Nikki cut her off, "Ni, we are so not going to have a scripture war right now. Do you want some thing to drink before we go?"

"What you got in there?"

"The usual...lemonade, red cool-aid, sprite, water, milk."

"Well I guess I'll have the usual, but easy on the sprite. My skin has been bad lately."

"Sprite and lemonade it is. " Nikki went to the kitchen calling behind her, "Do me a favor and go in my room and grab my white purse off the back of the door."

Benita got up and went up the stairs. She went into the bedroom and grabbed the white purse she had been sent for and opened the closet in search of a belt to match her outfit. Se had lost some weight and her jeans were sagging just a little. She called down to Nikki, "Hey, can I borrow a belt?"

Nikki didn't hear her but Ni knew she was welcome to any accessories she needed. The two more or less shared one expansive wardrobe in two homes and Ni browsed through the collection of belts. She considered taking her own red belt to wear but decided not to since it looked so good with Nikki's red boots and hat and she wasn't going to go through the trouble of changing her shoes. She grabbed a silk rainbow striped scarf and went back downstairs .

Nikki was waiting for her at the door with a foam cup in hand. "Why didn't you grab your red belt? It would look cute with that outfit."

"I know but I couldn't bear to break up the little red trinity you got going on with the hat and those boots."

"Well why didn't you just wear all three together?'

"What is this twenty questions? I didn't feel like changing my shoes!" Nikki looked down at Benita's flip flops. Before she could say anything Benita explained, "I didn't feel like looking in your sock drawer for socks and tying boots and the whole nine okay? Plus, you can rock boots all year. It doesn't really work for me. Especially boots like those."

"Boots like those? What does that mean?"

"Nothing bad, just snow boots. Or I should say winter boots. Timbs are snow boots aren't they?

"I don' know. I haven't seen enough snow to know what people wear when it snows and what they don't. Who is driving?"

"Me." Benita took her keys from her purse. "Now about this date tonight with your little devil friends..."

"Watch it Ni. Those judgments always come

back to haunt you."

"Look Nik, you knew me when I was a sinner. You know I'm not one to try to play like I'm perfect but sin is sin and when you are in it you are in it. There is nothing cute or nice about it and I'm not going to pretend there is."

"Yeah well you still have a tendency to be harsh and judgmental and it's not cool. Erin and Lisa are cool people and believe it or not they are Christian."

"What? How in the world can they be Christian?"

"What do you mean how can they be Christian? They believe Jesus is their Lord and savior."

"Well that's nice but you can't be a Christian and live in sin Nikki. To be a Christian means to be Christ-like and He did not live in sin."

"Yeah well he also didn't go around insulting people and judging them. He loved people no matter what they were into. He hates sin but he loves sinners. And the last I knew you you weren't perfect. Unless some thing happened in the last ten seconds that I missed you are a sinner too."

"Lets not have this debate today okay? Just be careful who you let get comfortable in your home. One day it's just dinner and the next thing people are spending the night and then you never know who might come waltzing up the stairs in the middle of the night with lust in her eyes. I'm not being funny. I'm being serious. Be careful."

Nikki knew Benita was trying to look out for her welfare so she didn't say anything else about her guests.

Chapter Three

As Lisa pulled in front of Nikki's home she was not happy. Erin had been a little too excited about Nikki. As Erin went on convincing Joshua how wonderful Nikki was, Lisa became more and more irritated. Lisa didn't say anything but she made a mental note to keep her eye on her girlfriend when she was close to NIkki. She had not sensed any sexual energy between them when they were together but still, some thing told Lisa that Nikki was somehow drawing Erin away from her. Lisa had no intention of letting that happen.

Joshua was nervous and kept asking, "Are you two sure she'll like me? You know I'm not real good with rejection."

Lisa was as irritated with his repeated question as she was with Erin's bragging about Nikki. "Joshua! If she doesn't like you so be it. There are other women out there. Just look at it as an opportunity to meet a new friend if nothing else."

"Yeah," Erin added, "She's real cool. I'm sure you two will get along great right honey?" She sat up in the back seat and put her hand on Lisa's shoulder and looked at her in the rear view mirror. She felt Lisa's tense attitude and not knowing what the problem was she decided not to ask until later on when they got home.

Lisa answered, "Yeah babe, she's real cool."

When they got out of the car Erin stretched, "I've never ridden in that back seat before. It is really not the most comfortable seat in the world."

Lisa shot her a look, "Yeah well it beats your beat up little ride."

Erin had been driving the same car since college and Lisa had been trying for years to convince her to get a new one. While Erin had given all sorts of reasons for not buying a new car it boiled down to one thing...sentiment. She had purchased her VW on her own at a time when her parents were using money to control her. There was nothing wrong with the car although she had put a bit of money into it a few times to keep it running. Every time she had to so much as change the oil Lisa tried to convince her that the car wasn't worth putting a penny into. The more Lisa complained about the car the more attached to it Erin grew.

How could she give up a car that had been the single most defining milestone in her independence because someone else wanted her to? Erin knew she'd be driving that Jetta for another 15 years if Lisa kept up her complaining about it.

As Erin was about to knock on the door it opened. Benita stood in front of them smiling. It wasn't the most genuine smile but it wasn't entirely fake either. Benita was smiling because she was glad to be there when they showed up, not because she was happy to see them.

Erin took a step back, "Oh, is this the right house? I am looking for Nikki."

"Oh, yeah, this is the right place." Benita extended her hand and introduced herself but neglected to invite them in. "I am Nikki's best friend, Benita...we are *platonic* best friends." Nikki pulled the door open wide and smiled, "Hey everybody! Come on in!" Benita noticed Joshua and a smile overtook her. She was a sucker for freckles. As everyone made polite introductions Nikki asked Benita if she was going to stay and dine with them. She knew Benita had stayed helping out per her request but she also knew she had dusted slowly to be there when her guests arrived.

Benita caught Joshua's eye and bashfully accepted the invitation. She was not pleased with herself for going all coy and cutesie. She was present as a warrior and this was no time to be making friends with the devil or flirting with any friends the devil might have sent to distract her. Nikki noticed Benita's flirtiness and was relieved. There was nothing about Joshua that even remotely attracted Nikki to him. He was too freckly for one thing and he was not gruff enough. Nikki was more

of a fan of manly men. She wasn't into the whole metro

sexual thing. Men who go get manicures and who take

longer in the bathroom getting dressed than women

confused her. She didn't like how hard it was to tell them

apart from gay men. As she contemplated manly men

she remembered the time she had gotten a shock once on

the beach.

~   ~   ~   ~   ~   ~

As she talked all afternoon to a guy who was as

gruff and manly as she would have any man be along

came another gruff manly man who pinched the guy she

had been talking to on his butt and said "Okay babe. Lets

get out of here. I think I'm ready for something to eat."

Nikki knew Miami was considered the gay

capitol of the world and she had no questions as to why.

~   ~   ~   ~   ~   ~

But Joshua showed no signs of homosexuality as he

barely took his eyes off of her as she moved about

tending to her guests. She knew he was desperate for attention and while he was very smart, funny and seemed to be kind he also seemed to Nikki to be insecure and wimpish.

Benita called to Nikki from the upstairs bathroom, "Hey Nik, can you come up here for a moment?"

Nikki excused herself and went to see what her friend needed. "What's up Ni? Why are you way up here? What's wrong with the powder room downstairs?"

"Shhh! I came up here so we can talk."

"Oh oh, here we go."

"No, it's not like that. I was just wondering what you think of Joshua?"

"Ni, you know me. You know all those freckles and all that soft spoken gentle guy stuff doesn't work for me. He's nice I guess but uh uh...not for me."

"Really? I think he's cute."

"Yeah, me too. A little too cute. If I want cute I'll

go to work and sit some body on my lap for a conversation. I don't like cute men Ni. You know that."

"Yeah. I do know that. Too bad. He seems really nice."

Nikki wanted to suggest Benita get his number or some thing but she knew with Benita it was best to let her come up with her own ideas. Someone else suggesting even what she wanted very badly to do was a sure way to get Benita not to do it. Nikki sighed, "So is that all Ni?"

"No. About the women."

"Yeah, what about them?"

"I think Erin is cool but that Lisa keeps giving you the mean face. Did you notice?"

Nikki was not about to entertain Benita's suspicious tendency. "No Ni. I did not notice. She's cool too. She's just not as soft as Erin, it takes her a little while to warm up to people I think."

"No Nik. That woman has a problem with you.

Every time Erin says some thing to you she eyeballs her all hard. And every time you say some thing to Erin she does the same."

Nikki opened the bathroom door and went out saying, "Not now Ni. Lets go enjoy ourselves shall we?" She started down the stairs and Benita followed close behind her.

In the living room the guests were flipping through the latest issue of Better Homes and Gardens. Joshua commented, "They always do such a wonderful job with the makeovers but I think most people can do the same if they just spend a little cash and some time thinking things out."

Lisa disagreed, "No way man. I can't do all that frilly fluffy decorative mess. I just don't have it in me."

Joshua shook his head at her, "It's not all about frilly fluffy Lisa. There are very masculine aspects and styles of decorating, clean lines, deep colors, metals and dark woods. Leathers, geometric shapes and hard angles.

Decorating is not all about floral prints and lace."

Benita was impressed. Nikki was not. Lisa shook her head and reminded Joshua, "You are talking to a woman who doesn't even pick out her own clothes to wear...right honey." She winked at Erin who wasn't sure why the wink made her uncomfortable. Nikki went into the kitchen and called out, "Hey dinner is ready. Does anyone want to help me set the table outside? Someone else can go into the little closet out there and light some citronella candles that are in there. The lighter is in there too."

Erin stood up, "I'll set the table. I like women's work." She entered the kitchen not noticing the unhappy expression on Lisa's face.

Joshua stood up, "I guess the closest thing to men's work is the candles. Where am I going?" Benita stood up more enthusiastically than she wanted to appear and was even more betrayed by her self when she nearly fell over Lisa trying to get by. "Oh, excuse me Lisa. I wasn't paying attention to where I was stepping."

Lisa was amused. She had already sensed that Benita was not a fan of hers and the fact that she almost ended up in her lap where she might catch whatever cooties she was s afraid of was a satisfying thought. Benita recovered effortlessly and offered, "I'll show you where to go Joshua but give me a minute." She grabbed her purse and went into the powder room. Opening her purse she pulled out a small vial of olive oil and anointed her legs. "Lord, please don't let any spirits transfer from that woman onto me. In the name of Jesus...Satan The Lord rebuke you!" She put the vial back in her purse and went to show Joshua where to find the candles. As they were close together in the small mud-room leading to the back patio Joshua commented, "Whatever she cooked smells great. Lots of olive oil. Must be a Mediterranean dish."

~   ~   ~   ~   ~   ~   ~   ~

The meal was perfectly prepared. By the time the group had finished eating the mood had taken a subtle turn towards nostalgia. The group shared stories of childhood and the difficult but oh so hilarious in hindsight teen years. Laughter was full and so was the group of unlikely friends. When a lull in the laughter and talk settled Lisa broke the silence with an offer, "Hey. I have a case of beer in the trunk of my car. I bought it for tomorrow night. We are having a little get together at my sister's house."

Nikki asked, "The one who told on you when you stole the gum from the gas station or the one you pushed down the stairs on prom night?" The group laughed together as Lisa answered, "The one I pushed...wait a minute! I swear I didn't push her! I stumbled and I was trying to catch myself! Come on man!"

Erin added, "Yeah, sure honey. That's probably why she only half speaks to you now."

Lisa answered, "No. You are why she only half speaks to me now. I told you she isn't into the whole alternative lifestyle thing."

Benita cut in under her breath, "Yeah well who with good sense is?"

Lisa frowned and rolled her neck slightly, "Excuse me?"

"You heard me. No offense but you have to know most people with good sense aren't going to accept that mess."

"Mess? What do you mean mess? You're a mess with all that hatred up in you calling yourself a Christian. I see all the hateful looks you keep throwing around here."

Nikki tried to calm them down, "Ladies. Ladies, please. This is a friendly affair. Ni, chill."

"Me chill? She called me hateful!"

Lisa slipped in, "You are hateful...tell the truth and shame the devil right?"

Joshua tried to calm Lisa, "Come on man, relax.

It's not a big deal. I've heard you called worse...shoot, I've called you worse myself. Remember the time I called you a fungus among us when you got ringworm from that weekend at the beach and you didn't speak to me for weeks?" Erin remembered it and smiled. His comment had not had the softening effect he desired on Benita as she whispered, "More like the plague."

Nikki was getting angry with Benita and stood up demanding, "Look. This is my house and I am not having this in here. Now five minutes ago we were all getting along fine and now you two want to act like a couple of fools and ruin a great night. Benita, to be real, you weren't even invited to this little diner party so if you have to continue in all that judgmental mean name calling you don't have to stay."

"What? Are you serious? I can come and clean up for your new friends but when things don't go how you want them to I can just go huh? That's deep Nik." She stood up and was preparing to go. She tried to hide the fact that she was both hurt and embarrassed but Erin felt it and tried to help, "Come on Benita, don't go. It doesn't have to be like that. We can talk about some thing else."

Lisa's face showed fury, "What? Don't go? What the hell is going on here?"

Benita blurted, "You aught to know that word...your future home."
Nikki snapped, "Ni go home! Oh my goodness! What is wrong with you?'

"Wrong with me?"

Lisa's voice was loud, "Yeah wrong with you! You think you can pick and choose who goes to hell? That's what's wrong with Christians. More of you will be in hell than homosexuals!"

Benita laughed hard, "Yeah right. It's a shame for you Erin. I can see on your face you know better than this mess. I'm happy to go home. If the skies crack open tonight this is not where I want to be sitting. I missed revival at First Baptist for this mess too. Nik, I don't know how I feel about you right now. You really just cut my throat I'm going to have to pray on that." She gathered her things and left as Nikki called behind her, "I'll call you later. We need to talk Ni."

Erin was sad. She felt a connection with Benita and was sorry she was leaving. Lisa saw her sadness and asked in an accusatory tone, "What's wrong with you?"

"Nothing Lis."

"No really, if anybody here should have that face it should be me. I can't believe you asked her to stay after she said what she said about us."

"About you Lisa. You two were going at it. She was nice to me."

"Nice to you? She said you were going to hell!"

"Maybe that's her way of being nice. Some people really care about the souls of others. They just don't know how to show it...like your sister."

Nikki took a deep sigh, "Lisa, I'll take one of

those beers if you don't mind."

Lisa stood up and cut a hard look towards Erin, "Yeah sure. They are warm though."

"It's cool. I have waterless ice cubes."

Joshua asked, "What is a waterless ice cube?"

As Lisa left the room she looked back at Erin to suggest she follow her. Erin tried hard to ignore Lisa. She did not want to get trapped out front in an argument. Nikki explained as she headed inside, "Waterless ice-cubes are little plastic shapes that are filled with water. You freeze them and put them in your drink. They cool your drink without diluting it."

Joshua had seen them before and nodded in recognition. As Nikki went inside Erin began to clear the table. Joshua smiled and whispered to her, "This doesn't help your dilemma does it?"

"You know Josh, it really doesn't. It seems like no matter where we go she has some problem with somebody. She's been gay her whole life. You'd think she'd know how to handle that kind of scrutiny by now. But she always blows it up and makes a huge scene. It's so embarrassing I'm tired of it Josh."

"I know you are. But you love her and if you were going to leave her you would have done so last year or the year before that, or the year before that..or the..."

"You know that Josh, I'm not so sure about that. It's all sinking in. We had this whole ceremony planned. So many people who I love will not be there. Did I tell you my mom has called a fast with all her girlfriends? They have been fasting for 12 hours a day since she got the invitation and she says they wont quit until I'm free."

"Free huh?"

"Yeah. Free. Imagine that."

Lisa came in the front door leaving it open behind her. Benita followed her in and called to Nikki, "Yo Nik!" Lisa went straight out back.

"Yeah! Ni? What's up? Did you realize you were

out of line and now you want to chill for the rest of the night? I hope so."

"Yeah, right. I see the after party is about to get started. Since when do you drink beer Nik?"

"You know I have a glass of wine every now and then."

"Like I said, since when did you drink beer?"

"Ni, come on. I don't think Jesus is going to disown me for having a beer."

"Never mind. I forgot the jacket for Sunday. The white one that goes with the lace skirt."

"Which one, the one with the lace or the other one?"

"The other one. I don't like all that lace together on me. It looks fine on you but on me it's a little too frilly."

"You know where it is. Go on up and get it."

Benita went up the stairs and into Nikki's room. The window was open and she could hear the conversation going on out back. She listened intently as she searched for the shoes that went with the jacket she was borrowing.

Erin defended herself, "It's not that Lisa. I just hate when you have to go and upset everyone we meet. It's like the only friends you want are the same ones you have had all your life."

Lisa denied bitterly, "That's bull E. We have met lots of people since we have been together!"

"Yeah but only gay friends."

Joshua cleared his throat loudly and Erin apologized, "My bad Josh. Let me say gay women and one straight man. Joshua is the only straight person in our lives. Don't you think that's odd?"

"No. Straight people hate us Erin. You saw that chick in here tonight. Oh yeah, I forgot, you wanted her to stay and abuse me some more."

"I didn't want either of you to act like you did but I did like her. She reminds me of my sister, and your sister...both of whom I really like."

"Where are they Erin? You don't see them knocking down the door to hang out with us. They are the ones who never come around. I never banned them from our lives."

Joshua excused himself and went inside to help Nikki with the dishes.

Lisa pulled Erin's chair close to hers and spoke in a tender voice, "Babe, what do you want me to do? It's not my fault they don't come around is it?" She tried to snuggle up to Erin but Erin pulled away and scooted her chair back to it's original place. Lisa's face was more than angry. It was threatening. "Oh? Is that how it is? I upset your holy roller buddies and now you can't even sit near me?"

"It's not that Lisa. This is a Christian home. I don't think all that is appropriate And if you were not always trying to throw our relationship up in people's faces they might come around more."

"What? Go to hell Erin. If I was a man it would be fine for me to get close to you when people are around."

Erin snappd at Lisa, "You know what Lisa, if I keep this up I just might go to hell! That's the root of the problem isn't it? You don't believe it but what if it is true? What if we are dragging one another to hell?"

"If there even is a hell you can believe there are worse people on earth to fill it with than me. I work hard, I'm a good person. I care about people, I am generous, I don't hurt people. I've been gay all my life. God made me this way."

"We don't have to end up how we start out Lisa."

Lisa pulled Erin's chair close again, "Babe, what's up? What is this? She really got to you huh?"

Erin didn't move her chair but she was very obviously not responding to Lisa's attempts to get close, "It's not her Lisa. It's this...this lifestyle. I love you. You are a better girlfriend than I ever had a boyfriend. But it's too much. Gay this gay that. Rainbow bumper stickers, rainbow, this rainbow that. People sneering. People fasting and praying...it's all too much."

"What do you mean? We have a right to be proud of who we are."

Erin whispered, "Pride is a sin."

Lisa didn't quite hear her and asked, "What was that?"

Erin changed the subject, "Lisa did you know what a rainbow is a symbol of?"

"Yeah. Gay pride what about it?"

"No. It's not about gay pride. After The Lord flooded the earth in Noah's time he gave the rainbow as a sign that he would never wipe out all of mankind that way again."

"So what are you saying?"

"Nothing."

"No really. What are you saying Erin?"

" I just think it's ironic that the symbol of God's

promise has become a banner for a sin against Him. It's like throwing that rainbow back in God's face and saying, "We can do what we want because you promised not to kill us all!"

"E, you're tripping." Lisa laughed nervously for a moment and then her face showed fury again, "Erin, if this is what I think it is, you better think again before you say anything you'll regret."

Nikki came out with glasses full of waterless ice, "Hey ladies. Where's the beer? I need something to relax me right now. This has been a tense evening. I don't know what got into Benita. She's a little anal sometimes but she's really cool."

Lisa opened the case of beer and stated, "That woman is a witch with a B where the W belongs. You can't apologize for her."

Nikki didn't like the insult to her friend who was not present to defend herself and she was glad Benita hadn't heard it. "She is my best friend and I don't appreciate you calling her names. She has been through a lot in her life and she has a lot to learn about grace but she has a good heart. I can't believe she acted like that though. She knows I don't like arguing in my home. I like peace."

Upstairs Benita stepped away from the window and found the shoes , grabbed the jacket and sneaked down the stairs and out the door.

Joshua took a sip of his beer and stated, "I liked her a lot. You're right, she has a lot to learn about grace but I really did like her. I like people who are committed to what they believe in. I like people who will stick to their guns. She was like a pit-bull!"

Lisa added, "She looked like one too."

Nikki was offended again but before she could respond Joshua did, "No Lisa. She was stunning. Those eyes, are you kidding? I've never seen eyelashes that long and judging from the fact that she wasn't wearing make-up I'd guess that they are real." He looked to Nikki for confirmation.

Nikki smiled glad for his support, "Yes they are real. If there is one thing anyone could say about Ni it's that she's real."

Chapter Four

At work on Monday Nikki and Erin talked about
how crazy things had been since dinner on Friday.
Benita had been all but harassing Nikki to get Joshua's
phone number from Erin.

~   ~   ~   ~   ~   ~   ~   ~

Lisa had been so extra sweet to Erin she thought
she'd end up with a few cavities just from being around
her. Lisa had even washed Erin's car Saturday morning,
which was a task Lisa emphatically insisted the two do
together as a couple since they had been together. It had
caused problems in the past when Erin didn't think her
car particularly needed to be washed while Lisa was a
car washing fanatic. They would argue about whether it
is selfish to insist someone else wash their car just
because you want to wash yours or if it was foolish not
to wash and wax a car regularly to keep it in perfect
condition. The argument always ended the same

way...with Erin rearranging her plans for the day to squeeze car washing into her schedule. But this past weekend Lisa had washed, waxed and vacuumed Erin's car long before Erin had even gotten out of bed.

By the time Erin got up Saturday morning she was awakened by the wonderful smell of beef bacon sizzling away downstairs. Lisa had prepared a huge and delicious breakfast which she insisted Erin eat in bed where she could relax.

Benita had been questioning Nikki all weekend about whether or not she was sure she had no romantic interest in Joshua. Benita just couldn't believe Nikki was going to pass up the opportunity to date such a clean cut, well spoken, well mannered, and oh so cute guy. "Nikki," She had reasoned, "even with the freckles you have to admit he is really hot! He's smart, laid back, come on, you have to admit the guy is quite a catch! And I think the freckles make him even hotter to be honest!"

Nikki admit, "He's quite a catch for some body,

maybe for you, but for me, I'd throw him back into the sea and try again any day of the week. But you can date him Ni, really, I don't think there is anything wrong with it. It was a blind date. It's not like we were actually dating. I think it was divine intervention that you stayed."

~   ~   ~   ~   ~   ~

Erin was more than happy to pass Joshua's number along to Benita. She knew it would make the fact that Nikki had no interest in him of little significance in the scheme of things. And if there was one thing Erin knew was no party it was dealing with Joshua when a woman rejected him. He wasn't prone to pouting. On the contrary, he went on and on about how stupid or blind or ignorant the women had been not to see a good man when he was right in front of her. There was no convincing him that it was a matter of taste, of fate, of divine purpose or anything other than the sad state of women in America.

Nikki called Benita to give her the number while Erin called Joshua to let him know Benita would be calling. Both Nikki and Erin were feeling quite accomplished when they got off the phone. They high fived and got back to work.

Benita called Joshua at lunch time and he answered right away. Both of them were nervous, which was characteristic of Joshua but not of Benita. She figured it was because she was typically the one getting the initial call from a perspective boyfriend, not making the call to one.

With a shaky voice she asked, "Hello. Is this Joshua?"

With equal nervousness manifest as cracking of his voice rather than the shaking she had exhibited he answered, "Yeah, um, yes it is, who am I speaking to please?"

"Hey this is Benita. Nikki's friend. Do you remember me?"

"Of course I remember you. Between those eyelashes and that attitude how could I forget you?" He immediately regret mentioning her attitude. He hadn't meant it in a bad way but he wasn't sure how she had taken it. He tried to explain, "By attitude I mean confident and assertive...not..."

"Never mind. I'm not offended."

"Oh good. Forgive me. I'm a little nervous so I might decide to taste my foot a little" He thought, "Did I just tell her I am nervous? What is wrong with me? And taste my foot? She'll think I'm out of my mind!"

Benita thought it was cute that he was so nervous he had to tell her about it. She also thought it was cute how he had put his own little spin on the cliché. She giggled and answered, "Hey, a little foot every now and then keeps one humble I think."

Joshua was relieved as Benita went on, "So I know this is awkward for me to call you when you were set up on a blind date with my best friend huh?"

"Well, I don't think it's awkward. No offense but your buddy is not all that dynamic. She's beautiful, there's no doubt about that. She's just a little reserved for my taste. I'm so laid back I need a woman who isn't afraid to pull me out of my shell to have some fun...not that I am suggesting you are my woman...I mean, you could be...well...eventually...or if you wanted..."

Benita saved him from his self, "Josh, relax! You really are nervous huh? It's cool. You were so relaxed the other night. It didn't seem like you were uncomfortable at all then."

"Yeah well when Nikki and I didn't particularly hit it off it was just like being with regular friends, a couple of new friends but just friends no less. But this is different. I'm not at all used to women calling me to initiate anything. I usually have a speech together for what to say on the first call and everything."

"Really? Guys actually do that whole speech preparation thing?"

"I don't know about other guys but I do...in the mirror and all, which is kind of stupid given the fact that you can't see a person through the phone."

"Well if it's a camera phone you kind of could"

"Yeah, and there are those George Jetson computers now too. Video calls through email accounts and everything… it's crazy."

"Yeah, you're right. So keep practicing in front of the mirror. It might come in handy sooner than you think."

The two laughed a little and then there was a brief silence before they both spoke at the same time saying the same words "So do you want to get together sometime?" They laughed again. Benita answered, "I guess I'll slip into my proper role here and let you be the aggressor. Yes, I would love to get together some time soon. I'm pretty much available in the daytime. I'm a nurse and I typically work in the evenings and nights through the week. I only work one weekend a month. So if you want to wait until the weekend that's cool but if you want to get together sooner it will have to be a lunch date. It's up to you."

Joshua was glad she had mentioned getting together sooner. He would have thought it was too aggressive to suggest anything that soon although he wanted to see her ASAP. "Well," He thought for a moment contemplating how far out on his shaky limb he was going to scoot, "How about tomorrow for lunch? If that's not too soon."

"It's perfect. What time do you take lunch?"

"I can take my lunch whenever .The assistant director will cover for me. Truth be told I do a lot of running around during the day. What time works for you?"

"Lets say 1. That way I can come home, catch a

nap, get myself together and then we can take our time and chill. Where do you want to go? Shall we meet up somewhere or are you a traditional guy and feel like it's not a date unless you pick me up at my house?"

"Oh, I know it's a date! It's up to you. It might be nice for me to pick you up so you can relax and not have to drive. I know you said you'll be taking a nap but still, why not relax and be rested as much as you can. I know all about night shift. I used to work at a convenience store at night. I remember those days...trying to get sleep but needing to get things done during the day. It's not easy."

"I love it. I have my system in order and I've been doing it so long it doesn't bother me at all anymore. But it would be nice not to have to drive if you don't mind picking me up."

"I'd love to. Just tell me where you live and I'll put it in my GPS and be there at 1."

Benita gave him her address and they both

expressed how they were looking forward to the next day.

Benita called Nikki who was tickled to see her friend so excited. "Ni...wow...you really are excited about him huh?"

"Yes! I really am. He was so cute on the phone trying not to taste his foot as he put it."

"Taste his foot? What kind of talk did you two have? Gross!"

"Jive you Nik. I thought it was cute. Anyway, I need you to help me figure out what to wear tomorrow. You know I haven't been on a date in a long time. I'm out of practice."

"Girl, just throw something on. You dress well everyday so it doesn't matter what you put on. I'd say do a skirt or a dress but other than that...you can handle it. If anyone can handle the fashion department it's you. If you need anything from my house you know the deal."

"Is my red and yellow dress over there?"

"Yeah, I just had it dry cleaned. I meant to give it back to you this weekend before I was tempted to wear it again. Then you'd be waiting another month for me to remember to take it to the cleaners."

"Girl please. I told you I throw that thing in the washer on delicates, hang it to dry and iron it on low."

"It's one thing if you ruin your clothes. It's another if I do. Anyway it's there and it's clean. You want to go get it or do you want me to bring it by later on. I do have to go home before I go out to the library for that book signing."

"Oh I forgot about that! That's tonight?"

"Yeah. I can't wait. Dawn Smith is my favorite poet. She has been since I was in junior high school. I can't believe she is coming to our library."

"Maybe I'll tag along....no, you know what... no I wont. If I'm going to do lunch to morrow I'll need a full rest tonight. I'll just go by your place and get the dress myself."

"Whatever works for you, but I can bring it by on my way to the library."

"Oh yeah, you did say that. That's even better. Thanks. And don't forget your red espadrilles. Oh. Never mind, I bought those red shoes the other day. I can wear them."

"You sure? The espadrilles go great with it. I'll bring them just in case."

"Okay. Thanks."

"Sure. Talk to you later."

"Love ya."

"Love you too."

Chapter Five

The next day Erin sat in the office of Sweet Blessings Daycare on the phone all morning. Lisa could not believe she had passed Joshua's number on to judgmental Benita. Erin tried to explain that it was not her fault that the two wanted to date but Lisa insisted that there was something she could have done to dissuade Joshua from going out with Benita. Lisa insisted, "Come on Erin, you know that man hangs on your every word. Why would you hook him up with someone who is going to insult you every time we get together as a group? That was just stupid!"

Erin was offended, "Stupid? You know it's funny how angry you get when people look at your life and pass judgment but you are so quick to try to control other peoples' lives. If he wants to date her I wish him and her the best. I like the woman myself. Sure she's a little overboard with her religion but I think she means well."

"Means well? She said we were going to hell Erin!"

"Yeah, and? Lots of people warn other people when they are on a path that won't lead to a good place. It's the ones who don't warn you that you need to watch out for."

The two had been arguing on and off all morning and Erin just wanted peace. She was thrilled when one of the teachers came and tapped on the door to remind her that she needed to make rounds to let a few people go on break. With a short and brisk tone Erin stated, "Look Lisa, I have to do breaks. I'll talk to you later."

"Yeah, how convenient. I'm calling Joshua to see if I can convince him to reschedule for never."

"Lisa...don't..." Click. Lisa hung up the phone in Erin's ear. As angry as Erin was that Lisa had hung up on her, she was more relieved to be of the phone. She left the office and said a small prayer for Joshua, "Lord. Please don't let him answer the phone. Let him have a nice date and maybe actually end up with a regular girlfriend."

~　　~　　~　　~　　~　　~　　~

It was 12:57. Benita stood in the mirror contemplating her shoe options. The espadrille was so accidentally sexy while the nine west sandal was quite intentionally sexy. It was a hard choice to make and she was still wearing one of each shoe when the doorbell rang. She went downstairs to answer it and was delighted to find Joshua standing there in a pair of Khakis and a red polo shirt. He was equally glad to see her in her red dress. "Hello lady! Wow, that's quite a beautiful color on you!"

"It doesn't look bad on you either sir."

Joshua looked down at Benita's feet and smiled, "Um..."

Benita smiled and explained, "Oh yeah, I was trying to decide which ones to wear. What do you think?"

Joshua answered without a pause, "The espadrilles, definitely. They are sexy but casual...like you didn't mean to be that sexy."

Benita was impressed that he had the same impression of the unintentional sexiness of the espadrilles and a little confused about the fact that he knew what an espadrille was. Joshua explained himself as if he had read her mind, "My mom worked in the fashion industry all my life. I know clothes. I know a pump from a kitten heel, a wedge from a platform, I even know an ankle boot from a shoe. If we get into my knowledge of fabrics we'll be talking for a week."

Benita shook her head and smiled, "You are an interesting person Joshua. I'll be right back." she hurried slightly up the stairs where she changed her shoe and grabbed her yellow beaded purse. She remembered when she found the blue purse at a yard sale. She was wearing the red and yellow dress that day and when she saw how perfectly the purse matched the embroidery on the dress she knew she had found a new friend. With one last glance in the mirror she left her room and went downstairs and out the door.

Joshua was waiting at his car holding the door open for her. She did not imagine him to be a Volvo man but she wasn't disappointed to discover that he was. It seemed everything about him was a pleasant surprise. It made her wonder what unpleasantness had kept him from having a wife or at least a steady girlfriend. As he got in the car she asked, "Okay, so you are well dressed, well spoken, well educated in fashion..."

He cut her off, "And business and the arts..." Benita rolled her eyes playfully, "Right, you probably have degrees in medicine, law and rocket science too huh?"

"No, but I did take first place in the science fair in second grade, as well as I am pretty well versed in homeopathic remedies and as for the law...well... I talked my way out of a ticket on the way over here...does that count?" They laughed together.

Benita decided, "Yeah, it counts. So tell me something...actually tell me two things..."

"Maybe."

"First, what made you decide to work in daycare?"

"That's a story I'll save for lunch. What's next?'

"Why aren't you married or at least in a relationship? You seem to have a lot going for yourself"

Joshua took a deep breath, "Same story. I guess I'll start talking."

He took another deep breath before explaining his painful past.

"I got married right out of high school. Lorena and I had dated since eighth grade. I loved her so much. Everyone knew we would get married and we did. We went to college together, she ended up having a baby while we were sophomores. People used to say how hard it must have been but it really wasn't. We were living our lives. Once the baby came she took her classes late in the afternoon and I took mine early in the morning. I worked nights as the manager of a convenience store to keep us afloat but we did have help from our parents and we had both gotten pretty hefty scholarships. Our parents kicked the money they didn't have to spend for our education our way to help out with our new family. It was really a wonderful life. By the time we graduated we had two kids, in fact Lorena gave birth to Madison weeks before graduation."

Benita was trying not to feel the regret she was feeling for getting involved with a man who had kids and an ex-wife. She was glad she had asked her questions on the first date. She figured she could get through this one date and move on. Benita was not in the market for step motherhood. When Joshua said his daughter's name Benita let go of her feelings of regret for a moment and commented, "Oh I love that name Madison."

Lorena named her. The deal we had made was

that she could name the girls if we had any and I could name the boys if we had any. Our son, Joshua, was born first. Lorena said she would have named him after me anyway so she actually got the better deal." Joshua smiled remembering Lorena and the kids. Lost in the memory he had paused for a long time.

Benita had to prompt him to continue, "So you have two kids at graduation and everything is going great..."

"Yeah. So after graduation I took another job with the same company as the general manager in another store. It paid well and Lorena stayed at home for a year with the kids. She loved it but I could tell she was getting a little bored staying home all the time. I suggested she get a part time job and she jumped on that.

"She started a job at a daycare center and that worked out good because the kids went with her to work. She loved it. We had a good life. Of course we had our ups and downs, like we had an ongoing battle over whether or not little Joshua would ever be allowed to join the military. Her dad was a colonel in the army. You know, we had our struggles and our bad times but in general, overall, we had a god life."

Benita could tell he was trying not to tell what went wrong. She didn't want to push but she did want to know. "So you're working for the convenience store as the general manager, Lorena works in a daycare center, the kids go to work with her, everything is swell..."

"Yeah, everything was perfect." He paused and Benita could see he was upset by whatever was coming next. She didn't want to ruin their first and last date so she assured him, "Look, you don't have to tell me what happened. I see it's upsetting you. Lets change the subject."

Joshua pulled the car over. Benita thought he was about to break into sobbing tears or something drastic but he turned to her and said, "Well, we're here. I guess I will tell the rest over lunch." He got out of the car and walked around to let Benita out. Benita was surprised at how close the restaurant was to her home. She had driven down this street enough times that she should have noticed the cute little venue.

Getting out of the car she exclaimed, "Oh wow! Look at this place it's adorable! It's like old world charm in the heart of Miami! I've never even noticed this place before...how odd."

"Yeah but you have heard of it haven't you?"

Benita knew she was about to be embarrassed but had to admit that she hadn't, "I really don't think so. What's it called?"

"Rino's. It's world famous...really. People come from all over to have their legendary traditional Italian food."

"Oh wait, is this the place that all the stars talk about?"

"Yeah."

"I never would have guessed it was right here.

You'd think it would be some where more...more..."

"Yeah I know closer to all the hot spots right? That;s part of it's charm. These guys aren't in it for all that. They have been here for generations making great food like their ancestors made it back home in what they call the old country."

The inside of the restaurant was as charming as the outside. Benita had never been to Italy but she felt like she had just stepped off of one continent and onto another when she walked in the doors. They were seated near a back window which looked out on a traditional Italian courtyard with lovely grapevines and all. Joshua explained, "They have their own wine that they press right here on the premises but they only sell it to people who come to eat here. For decades people have been trying to get them to mass produce it to sell but they won't do it."

"Is it any good?"

"It's the best I've had. We'll order some with our

meal."

"Don't you have to get back to work?"

"No. I took the rest of the day off. I wasn't sure how things would go with us. I didn't want to have to cut a great time short or have to go back and explain to the ladies at the center how bad things went if that ends up being the case."

Joshua ordered in Italian for both of them which Benita was surprised to find romantic. She just had to know how this man managed to lose his wife and kids. "Okay," she smiled resting her elbows on the table and her chin on her knuckles, "So life is perfect with Lorena, Little Joshua and Madison..."

"Right." The waiter set water in front of them with cut lemons on a tiny plate. Joshua took a lemon from the plate and squeezed some into his glass. He took a sip and continued his story, "Yeah. Then one day it all ended just like that." He took another sip of the water and said, "This water is even delicious, take a sip."

Benita was annoyed by his stalling but took a sip anyway. She was surprised at how good the water was. It was pure and cold and very refreshing. She took another sip...and another. Joshua smiled, "Try it with the lemon. Trust me."

"No, I'm not into lemon in my water."

"Try mine and see if you still feel that way."

Benita took a sip of his water and she was surprised at how much she liked it. Almost ashamedly she took a lemon and squeezed some into her own glass asking, "What do they do back there? I mean, if the water is this good I might pass out from the food."

As if on cue the waiter came and placed a basket of bread and a small portion of seasoned olive oil between the couple. He offered his damp towel to Joshua who cleaned his hands explaining, there is a mild cleaning agent on the towel, it will sanitize your hands.

Benita followed Joshua's lead noticing the fresh lemony smell of the cloth, "Lemony, what is it?"

Joshua smiled, "Lemon juice and water." Benita smiled and watched the server take the towel and toss it into a cute little basket. She had not noticed the tiny station with white towels stacked on a lovely shelf before. Benita began to grow upset with herself. How could she justify passing this guy up? He was the most romantic and wonderful guy she had ever met! She knew she was not cut out for step motherhood but Joshua was all that she ever wanted in a man and more. She desperately hoped his story would reveal some huge flaw in him that would justify her walking away and not looking back. At this point, his having two kids was losing it's offensiveness although his being divorced was still quite the turn off.

Joshua took another sip of his water and continued his story, "So one day I got home from work and I was surprised not to smell dinner cooking. It was not like Lorena not to have dinner started when I got home. Then I remembered that she had called me and told me she would be stopping by the mall to get Madison a few outfits and some shoes for Joshua. We had agreed to have Chinese take-out which she was going to pick up on her way home.

"I was antsy to see her come in the door but busied myself going through the mail. I figured it was just because I was used to coming home to her and the kids scurrying to me to give me love at the door. I sat down at the kitchen table and I just couldn't focus on the circulars. So I got up and put some water on for tea. I sat back down and before I knew it I was asleep. It was the strangest thing! I didn't even know I was asleep until the teakettle squealed and the doorbell rang at the same time.

"I jumped up and moved the teakettle from the heat and went to the door. When I opened it these two cops were there and I just knew something bad had happened. I didn't give them time to speak. I asked where my wife and kids were.

"The lady officer asked if she could come in for a

moment. She said I might want to sit down. I told her she could come in but that she needed to tell me where they were first. She looked into my eyes and said, "Sir, I'm so sorry."

Joshua was shaking and took a sip of his water, "It's like it was yesterday when I tell it. Those words. I knew. They were gone...all of them."

Benita was ashamed of herself. She had been waiting for this man to reveal his big flaw and he had revealed his greatest pain. She was expecting him to tell her he had done something horrible to drive his wife and kids away and all he had done was love them. "Oh, Joshua, I'm so sorry. I'm sorry I even asked."

The server came and set their food in front of them. Joshua lowered his head and prayed "Lord we thank you for your many blessings you have given us. We thank you for your plans for us. We thank you for this day and for the food we are about to eat. We ask that you will bless it and the hands that prepared it. In Jesus name, Amen."

Benita muttered, "Amen."

After a brief reverent silence Joshua shook off his somber mood and spoke with enthusiasm, "Okay so now you are about to take a taste of the finest cuisine in all of Miami with the exception of my mother's holiday cooking."

"Oh, just her holiday cooking? What about her regular everyday cooking?"

"My mother only cooks on special occasions. My cousin is my parent's personal chef. She does the everyday meals... and to be honest, I don't think she's all that skilled. All her food tastes the same to me. But my parents like it so who am I to complain right?"

"Right."

"So, anyway," Joshua continued the story showing a bit less pain, "after the accident I didn't know what to do with myself. I went back to school and more or less became a professional student for a long time.

Nothing seemed to take away the loneliness. I tried every hobby out there, I tried working all the time, I even tried drugs...thank God I didn't like being high and never got into it but I did try."

Benita was thoroughly enjoying her meal and Joshua. She wanted time to stand still so that she could sit in this adorably romantic moment forever, or at least for a few hours.

Joshua continued, "It wasn't until I met Lisa that I found something that helped. I met her at the gym. She just came up to me and started talking to me. I was annoyed. I could tell she was gay for one thing and I didn't particularly have any interest in developing any friendships with people living so called alternative lifestyles.

"But she never took the hint. Every time she saw me at the gym she would come and talk to me."

"About what?"

"Anything! Everything...she just attached herself

to me in a way. Before long I noticed I would look for her when I got there and one day she invited me to volunteer for the Special Olympics. I don't know why I said yes but I did.

"Thats where I met Erin and she noticed how good I was with the kids. She asked if I worked with children. I thought it was a ridiculous question. But I did notice I hadn't had time to feel sorry for myself when I was helping the kids and I had noticed how their smiled filled my heart.

"I started volunteering more and more and after a few months all I wanted to do was be around kids. I told Erin and Lisa that and Erin offered me a job in the daycare center she was running at the time...Potential Plus...where I am now.

"One of the mothers who had a serious crush on me bugged me every day to come to church with her and one day I did. I had no idea The Lord was waiting for me there. It was like as soon as I got in the sanctuary I knew

I had entered something...well, something special, some thing holy. I knew all the answers were there and I gave my life to Jesus that day.

"So here I am now with you feeling like something special is happening. I don't know what. I just know we'll be friends forever. You have such a good heart under all that anger and judgment."

"Anger and judgment?"

"Yeah, it's fear really. I can see it in your eyes. You're scared someone might see you and you're even more terrified that no-one will. But I do Benita. I see you."

Benita didn't know what to say. She was overwhelmed with emotions. His story was so unexpected. She had wanted to say something mean about Lisa but was somehow thankful for her. If she wasn't gay and trying to be all buff like a man where might Joshua be now? And if Joshua was seeing her for real he was sure to walk away. She had so many bad habits, of judging people, un-forgiveness, self righteousness, She was not unaware of these things within herself. She just didn't know how else to protect herself in this world full of devils.

Chapter Six

Summer Camp was starting and Nikki was excited. She loved doing all the fun summer activities with the kids. Water guns and water balloons, picking flowers and strawberries, taking the kids on trips to the zoo and days spent at the local pool were all parts of what made summer Nikki's favorite time of the year. Even though temperatures in Miami allowed for all those things all year, their curriculum during the school year didn't allow for so much free play time.

Nikki was also excited because Benita was finally going to offer first aid classes to parents at the center. Nikki had been trying to hook that up since last year but there was controversy over whether or not parents would take the classes without getting certificates of certification. In one week Nikki had recruited enough parents to call for two classes per week for the three weeks Benita was offering them. It helped a lot that Erin had also pushed for parents to sign up. She boasted on Benita as if the two had known one another for years and while Nikki did appreciate the support in recruiting enrollees for the class, she was a little uncomfortable with Erin pretending to know Benita so well.

Nikki put on her Khaki shorts and her Sweet Blessings Tee-shirt and left her house. She was surprised to find Lisa standing on the curb when she got outside. She had not seen Lisa since the dinner at her house and that was weeks ago. Lisa turned abruptly when Nikki came out the door, "Oh, Nikki, you startled me."

"Well, I assume you knew I would be coming out soon seeing as you are waiting here on the curb. Are you okay?" Nikki noticed Lisa's eyes were swollen as if she had been crying.

Lisa barked, "You know what Nikki, I'm not okay. I'm really not. Since we were here the other night things with us have not been the same. Erin talks about the Bible all the time and it's driving me crazy. Last night she slept on the couch because I had been flirting with her all day like I do when I want to...well, you know, make love. I don't know if she is going to break up with me or not but if she is I'd rather she do it and get it over with than string me along like this."

"Lisa, I'm on my way to work. I don't mean to be insensitive but this seems like it's going to be a long talk. Do you want to get together for lunch later and we can talk then? I really do have to get in on time today with the start of summer camp and all."

Lisa ignored Nikki's comments and continued her story, "It's just that she promised she would not leave me and now I think she is leaving and I have invested a lot in that girl. I have done a lot for her over the years. I was there for her when her dad died. They weren't on speaking terms and he got in a car crash and died. It was hard for her and I was there for her day and night. I was there for her when she lost the baby."

Nikki's expression showed confusion and Lisa responded to it. "Yeah, twice she has cheated on me. Once she ended up pregnant and had a miscarriage. I was there holding her hand at the hospital. How many people do you know who will be there for you when you cheat on them and get pregnant...to go to the hospital with you and let you cry all over them?"

"Not too many Lisa. It sounds like you've been a great friend to Erin. But really I do have to go. I hate to be insensitive but really…" Nikki started walking towards her car and Lisa followed her.

"No! No Nikki! I haven't been a great friend to her...I've been her girlfriend...I've been a great girlfriend to her. There is a big difference and that's the problem. Since we left your house she's been treating me like a friend and it's not cool!" Lisa's voice was loud and angry. Nikki was very uncomfortable with the accusatory tone she was using, "Lisa, I have nothing to do with that. But I really do have to get to work. Meet me for lunch at The Little Bistro. I take lunch at 1...nap time."

Lisa huffed and ran her hands through her hair and started to cry, "It's not fair. It's just not fair. If I had a dick this wouldn't be happening...excuse my language...but it wouldn't would it? If I was a man you would be here telling me how you'd talk to her and let her know she doesn't want to lose me after all I had done for her. Why is that different just because I'm a woman? What's the difference? The Bible says to love one another right? What's wrong with us loving one another?"

"Lisa, there are a lot of differences between men and women. There are reasons it's not condoned by God."

"No there aren't! Love is love!"

Nikki opened her car door and Lisa stepped back with a resentful look on her face, "You know what Nikki, I see you have more important things to do than be there for a friend who needs you. That's what Jesus would have done right? Just get in his car and go to work like any other day. I swear...you so called Christians." She turned abruptly and walked away. Nikki called after her, "Lisa, Lisa! Wait a minute. I want to help you if I can but lets just meet for lunch. 1 o'clock at the Little Bistro okay!"

Lisa got in her car without responding to Nikki at all. In her car Nikki prayed for strength and then started the car while dialing the number for Sweet Blessings. Erin picked up the phone "God morning, Sweet Blessings Christian Daycare Center, this is Erin Mayfield, senior director, how can I help you?"

"Good. It's you. Listen, I'm running a little late. I'll be there in ten minutes. I'm in my car pulling out from in front of my house now."

"Oh Nikki. Sure, that's fine. Just get here ASAP. There are kids all over the place! Your new assistant isn't here yet so your class is here in my office."

"In your office? Why don't you just wait in my room?"

"Clyde is cleaning up vomit in your room. One of the twins, the little girl, she got all upset when her mom left and she threw up all over the place."

"Ugh! Are you serious?"

"Yeah, apparently they had a big breakfast, but none got on the new carpet so that's good."

"You always find the silver lining don't you?"

"Not always but I had a good night's rest last night so I'm prepared for this day. See you when you get here. Hurry but drive safely."

"Okay. See you in a few."

They hung up and Nikki thought of how ironic it was that Erin's peaceful night of sleep was Lisa's seeming breaking point. She asked herself, "Should I have told her about Lisa? Oh well, I'll tell her later if I get the chance."

She most definitely got the chance later. Once everyone was settled in and had participated in the morning fun, eaten lunch and were all about to take naps Nikki heard some commotion coming from down the hall near the office. She left her assistant in the classroom and went to see what was going on. Lisa was outside the door banging hard on it and demanding that Erin open it. Erin talked to her over the intercom and explained that she was not going to let her in given her state and the fact that it was nap time. Two other teachers had gathered to observe the scene and Erin was obviously more than embarrassed She was mortified. She begged for Lisa to relax and be quiet so she could come outside and talk to her but Lisa kept yelling, "No you relax! I'll relax when you open the door!"

Nikki spoke to Lisa over the intercom, "Hey Lisa, it's Nikki. What's going on?"

"Oh now you want to talk to me. You didn't have much to say earlier when I needed to talk!"

Erin asked, "Earlier?"

Nikki explained, "Yeah. That's why I was late. I was going to tell you before I went to lunch. I didn't have time with the crazy morning we had."

Lisa's expression was blank. She did not want to show her jealousy. She thought it would have been simple to mention it when they were on the phone but she didn't say anything. Instead she threw up her hands and said, "Well since she wants to talk to you so bad why don't you calm her down." Lisa walked away and went into the restroom. Nikki opened the door and went outside nearly knocking Lisa over as she pushed the door open.

"Wow! Knock me down why don't you! What do you want?"

"I want to know what's up with you. Are you trying to get Erin fired? You know people talk around here. Now after all that mess she went through when she first mentioned you and now you want to come here and act up. The only reason the Bishop let her keep her job was because no-one could say you had ever come here and so there was no proof outside of rumors that she really was gay. Now I have to tell you if you were a man here doing this we would have long ago called the police. This kind of thing upsets kids...and women."

"Yeah whatever Nikki. The reason she has this job is because the last director accused that Bishop of sexual harassment and nobody else would touch this place with a ten foot pole!"

"Where did you hear that? That whole scandal was like 15 years ago! And I have spoken to people who were right here when it all hit the fan and I assure you the Bishop did no such thing. That woman had it in her head that she was going to marry Bishop Jones and when he got engaged to Minister Patty she flipped out. Don't believe everything you hear on the streets Lisa. And that was ages ago anyway."

"Yeah well why did she think he was going to

marry her? There had to be something going on for her to think that."

"Yeah, they had lunch a couple of times here in the office to discuss ordering new supplies and equipment. That was when the center fist opened. He didn't know what eh was doing. She helped him out a lot. Really that's all there was to it. She had in her head that she was going to marry him from the start. For years she told people he was her future husband. But Minister Patty came in out of the blue one day with a promise from the Lord. As soon as the Bishop met her he knew she was the one and from there it's all history…. Ancient history at that. If you want to know the real story ask someone who was around when it happened. But that's neither here nor there. Why are you here acting all crazy? You couldn't wait another ten minutes and meet me for lunch like we planned?"

"We didn't plan anything. You suggested it but I never said I would meet you."

"Okay whatever. So what are you going to do? Stay here banging on the door until one of the teachers calls the police on you?"

"If I have to yes I will. She can't just ignore me. She has to say something"

"Yeah well, that sounds nice and all but the truth is there is a steel door and a state of the art security system between you two. If she wants she really can ignore you. Even your banging on the door sounds like a little kid from in there."

"So how can I be upsetting the kids so much? You see, you Christians are so full of it!"

"You know what Lisa, I never bash gay people and you are not going to keep trash talking Christians, at least not to me. I've never been anything but nice to you and neither has Jesus. Now for your information every time you buzz the buzzer a little bell rings in the hallway...it's called a doorbell. And every time you talk into the intercom what would ordinarily only be heard from some one relatively close to the door is heard all throughout the center since you're yelling like you've lost your mind. Now this is my last attempt to help you and then I'm going inside and if someone calls the police so be it. Do you want to go to lunch so we can talk or what?"

Lisa hung her head in silence. After a moment Nikki raised her hand to push her four digit code on the keypad and Lisa stopped her, "Wait! Don't go inside. I'm sorry for all the Christian bashing. I do need to talk. Lets go to lunch. My treat."

Chapter Seven

Nikki was wondering why she was so nervous about the first aid classes. Benita had given them before at other places and she knew she would be great. The people who had signed up were all excited and Erin had ordered dinner for everyone and was excited too.

It was now Thursday and the drama from Monday morning had gone from hot gossip to old news. So far as Nikki knew Bishop Jones had not heard about it. She figured if he had she would have been one of the first people he would have contacted for details. Nikki had no idea what the status of Lisa and Erin was but she didn't ask any questions. She could tell she had somehow offended Erin in all of it so she kept her hands out if it as much as she could.

Erin didn't say she was offended and she never treated Nikki badly at work but she had not been as friendly lately as Nikki had gotten used to her being. Now she seemed to treat Nikki like everyone else which came to Nikki as a very relieving surprise. Her days at work were focused, simple, uneventful except for the many wonderful and funny things her kids did.

As Nikki sprayed down the last of the toys with organic disinfectant Erin came into her room. She sat down next to Nikki and handed her a small truck, "Nikki, you've been quiet lately. Everything okay? You seem distant these days."

Nikki didn't know how to answer. Everything was indeed fine but she knew that Erin was trying to open discussion up by way of projecting her feelings onto Nikki. She knew if she indulged the tactic it might end her up in a conversation she had no interest in being in. If she didn't indulge however, she might just miss an opportunity to minister to Erin by simply humbly loving her. Nikki decided to use tough love and not feed Erin's foolishness. "I'm fine. Just excited about this class tonight."

"Yea me too. The moms are all excited."

"Don't forget about Mr. James, Veronica's pop-pop. He's more excited than anybody I think."

"Yeah. I think so." There was a long silence before Erin continued, "Listen, I never said thank you for Monday."

Nikki nodded, "Oh sure. She was really upset. Apparently she hasn't slept alone in a long time. She said she couldn't sleep at all and that when she doesn't get sleep she gets all nutty. She apologized to me the next day."

Erin was possessive in tone, "Yeah, I know I was on the line with her. How do you think she got your number?"

"Oh, I didn't think of that."

There was another long pause. Nikki was not sure why she asked the next question but it fell from her lips before she could choke it back. "Are you two okay?"

Erin was possessive in tone again, "Yeah! We are fine. She's still mine if that's what you are wondering."

"Well, no, or… never mind. I was just asking. It seemed like she thought you two might be breaking up. She was really upset about that. She loves you a lot I guess."

"You guess? What is that supposed to mean?"

Nikki knew she had gotten into a mess she was not going to have an easy time getting out of. She tried to censor her words, "I mean, sometimes when we are in bad relationships it's hard to know the difference between loving someone and wanting to own them. I think you two have a connection but I'm not sure how much of it I'd call love...but that's not uncommon in relationships in general."

"So you see us have one little fight and you think

you can say she doesn't love me? She loves me and I love her. Make no mistake about it."

"I am sure. You two have been friends for a long time, You've been through a lot together."

"You and Benita have been friends for a long time. What Lisa and I have is different, special. Nobody is ever going to break up that love."

Nikki knew she was better off not saying much at all, "Okay. Well, I'm going to go and take a nap in my car before this class starts. I just got a new worship CD and it puts me to sleep in one minute. That gives me..." she looked at her watch "...twenty seven minutes." Both women stood up and left the classroom.

An hour later almost everyone who was scheduled to attend the class had arrived and were enjoying the dinner they had been provided. The grilled chicken Caesar salad was very gladly eaten. It was hot outside and although people were hungry no one wanted anything heavy. The cool crisp romaine lettuce and the perfectly juicy grilled chicken pleased the attendees and made for great conversation about how surprisingly easy it is to eat well. While there was a lot Nikki could have said about the importance of developing good dietary habits at a young age she kept her thoughts to herself.

She had not talked about her past battle with Bulimia in years and wasn't sure why it had even come to mind. Nikki didn't even allow herself to entertain the thought of it and made her way to the office to call the missing attendees. She met Erin on the way and asked if she had heard from any one else. Nikki was particularly interested in the whereabouts of Benita who had set up and gone out to get a cup of coffee almost forty minutes ago. The coffee shop Benita had gone to was only a few blocks away so Nikki was a little worried.

"Well," Erin informed her, "Benita is outside talking with Evelyn. I talked to Mr. James and he said he's feeling sick so he's not coming. I think everyone else is here right?"

"No. What about Jane Forbes and her new man. Aren't they coming?"

"Oh, no she called and asked if she could do next week's class. Benita said is okay so that's it for tonight." Erin abruptly walked away.

Nikki was actually glad not to have to make the calls since doing so was really only an intended distraction from thoughts of her past. Now she could go outside and chat for a couple of minutes before class. She went outside where she found Benita and Evelyn whispering on the far end of the porch. Evelyn was obviously uncomfortable with Nikki's presence but Benita showed no reaction whatsoever to Nikki's approach.

Benita continued what she had been saying "...Well I guess that never came up during the interview. I mean where does it fit in?"

Evelyn looked sheepishly at Nikki and contemplated saying more. Benita assured her, "Oh, Nik is cool. She's my best friend. She knows how I feel about it. We don't do the secret thing."

Nikki crossed her arms in disapproval, "Benita, are you out here telling people's business?"

Benita didn't play at remorse, "You know what I say, don't do it if you will be ashamed of it later. It's not like she's in the closet! She's the one who announced that she was going to get married! When are they doing to do that anyway?"

Nikki didn't really want to be a part of backbiting but she did feel a responsibility to tell what of the truth she could and put Evelyn at ease about the director of her children's daycare center. "I don't think they are still planning that. In fact I'm not sure how much longer they will be together. But none of that has anything to do with her job. She's great here and she's great with the kids. Her personal life is...uh personal...go figure!"

Evelyn squirmed and said with ambivalence, "But don't you think there should be some greater level of accountability in a Christian center? That's why I brought my kids here, because I knew it was a Christian center and that made me feel safe. If it's going to expose them to what the world has to offer then I may as well send them some where else, especially for the price."

Nikki was not about to let this witch hunt mentality prevail. "Evelyn, you live with your kids' dad and you aren't married right? Well if you are so concerned with them getting Christian values instilled in them you might want to consider your own lifestyle before you go trying to protect them from other people. I mean, lets be real here... who on this porch can say they are sin free?"

Benita looked at her watch and was not thrilled to realize there were only five minutes before class was scheduled to start, "I'll bet the Bishop doesn't know about her lifestyle though. If he did he would surely get her out of here. I like her. I think she's a cool person. But sin is sin and that's the bottom line."

Evelyn nodded her head, "Yeah, I'm not married but I don't work in a daycare teaching people's kids. If I mess my own kids up that's my business. She's messing up other people's kids. That's different."

Nikki was getting more than irritated, "I can't even address that right now. There are too many levels on which that is just wrong and faulty thinking. And as for you Benita, watch out with all that talk about other people's sin."

Benita was combatant, "What do you mean by that? I'm not perfect but I'm not living some lifestyle committed to sin!"

"Ni, all I know is you should watch the stones in your glass house."

"Glass house? What glass house? What are you saying? I live uprightly before The Lord..."

"All I'm going to say is just because you don't tell doesn't mean it didn't happen or that other people don't know about it."

The door opened suddenly and Erin peeked her head out, "Ladies, it's time for class. Are you coming in or do I have to start telling bad jokes to keep the people calm?"

The group followed her into the building and the rest of the evening went smoothly.

The next day when Nikki got to work Erin bolted out the door at her, "What did you say to Evelyn last night Nikki?"

"Hold on Erin! Good morning to you too! Geez! Can I get in the door before you verbally assault me with that accusatory tone?"

"Yeah, come in here and see me in the office once you clock in." Erin had never spoken to Nikki in such a demanding tone and Nikki had to stop herself from reminding Erin that she was from the ghetto and was just as likely to wipe the floor with her as she was to shake her hand. The truth was Nikki was not at all likely to do any physical harm to anyone anymore although there were times when she fondly remembered the days when she would have.

Nikki took a moment to pray while she clocked in and when she left the lounge she walked slowly to the office wondering what kind of twist the truth had taken to have Erin so upset. She muttered quietly before entering the office, "I'm going to kill Benita. Ugh!"

She entered the office and Erin, who was seated at her desk talking on the phone, pointed abrasively to the chair opposite her without so much as looking up at Nikki. Nikki sat down and prayed for patience while she waited. The conversation Erin was having made Nikki both sad and angry.

Erin explained, "Well sir, I am sure I didn't deceive you. The question you asked was whether or not I was living with a man who was not my husband. I specifically told you that I was living with my girlfriend." There was a brief pause and Erin shot a hostile look towards Nikki. "Well, I am sure I can't be held responsible for what you or anyone else assumed sir. The truth is I answered all your questions truthfully." There was another pause and Erin's head dropped in to her hand, "Yes sir, of course I am willing to go before the board. Just let me know when that will be." There was a short pause, "Oh that soon? Well of course I can make it. Yes. You too Bishop. I'll see you on Monday evening then. Yes. Okay. Thank you. I need all the prayer I can get." She hung up and held her head in her hands for a moment before looking up at Nikki with regretfully tearful eyes.

She choked back her vulnerability and hissed at Nikki, "What did you two tell Evelyn last night? I have been getting calls all morning from parents talking about they aren't sure they will be bringing their kids because of what they heard about my lifestyle! That was Bishop Jones I just hung up with! He heard I have been flaunting my homosexual behavior in front of the children! He got a call from Evelyn too I guess. Of course he won't say it was her specifically but I imagine it was since she apparently called every parent she knew with the hot gossip! What did you tell her?"

"What did I tell her? Nothing! I told her if she was going to judge people she better start with herself living with a man she's not married to!"

"You know what Nikki, I knew it was a mistake letting Benita come here. I knew something bad was going to happen. She was too nice to me. I should have listened to Lisa. She warned me about her but I didn't listen."

"Well Erin, you are the one who shared your sexuality with everyone here. You told everybody you were getting married to Lisa months ago! Did you think people were going to just forget about that? You can't blame anyone for this but yourself. Your lifestyle is your choice and the fact that you don't hide it is your choice too."

"The fact that I don't hide it? Why should I hide

it?"

"Well, face the music then Erin. It's your life, your choice. I've never done anything to you. Don't try to use me as your scapegoat. If you want we can pray..."

"You know what Nikki...you can keep your prayers to yourself." Erin picked up the phone and dialed and Nikki took the hint and got up to go. As she opened the door Erin said to her, "By the way, you can go home."

Nikki turned around, "Go home?"

"Yes. Go home. Not even half your class is here today. I think we can handle it without you. Take the day off."

Nikki wanted to protest but the Holy Spirit held her tongue. She simply left the room, walked to the lounge and clocked out. As she was leaving the lounge she overheard two of the other teachers whispering outside the door. They were laughing about how easy it was to get the moms to keep their kids home. One of the women mentioned, "Erin never should have fired her in the first place or she wouldn't be home to watch all those kids!"

Nikki shook her head. She did think it was a bit impulsive how Erin had fired Linda but she had no idea there was a whole conspiracy born that day to get back at Erin. That had happened months ago and Nikki had forgotten all about it. The two teachers talked a while about how long they thought Erin would last and Nikki boldly walked out in to the hallway where they were startled by her. "Ladies, do you think it is Christ like to go through all this to get some one fired? That is what you are doing right?"

Brandy, the younger of the two women answered, "I know she's your special little friend but the rest of us don't want to be here subject to some blatant sinner. The parents feel the same way."

Nikki shook her head and left. She stopped to get ice cream on her way home and spent the day watching the food network and munching on healthy snacks and ice cream.

Se was awakened from a nap that had sneaked up on her by her cell phone ringing . She answered it and was surprised to find it was Bishop Jones. He asked her if she would be able to meet with him for lunch some time before Monday so that he might get from her a better understanding of what was going on at Sweet Blessings before Monday's board review with Erin.

Nikki agreed and after taking a sip of her water went back to sleep.

Chapter Eight

Joshua and Lisa stood outside the gym together arguing playfully over who would buy lunch. Every Saturday the two played at the same ritual. They had bet that the first one showered and out the door would pick where to eat while the other paid. The two had come bolting out of their respective locker rooms and raced to the front door madly. Joshua had almost run over a young teenage girl and stopped to apologize and hold the door for her while Lisa made her way to the sidewalk out front.

Joshua agreed to pay if Lisa allowed him to select

where to eat. Knowing her friend she teased, "Yeah, but no dollar menus and no pizza!"

Joshua smiled widely, "Why would you say that Lisa? I'm a man who loves a good meal."

"Yeah, but lately you have been doing all your fine dining with your new girlfriend. You ain't gonna take me to no fast food dollar menu! "

"Guilty as charged. Where do you want to go?"

Lisa smiled back at him and admitted, "Actually, I really do have a taste for pizza!"

At Pizza World they sat in the small booth waiting for their broccoli, mushroom and onion pizza. Joshua asked Lisa, "So, what's going on with you and Erin?"

"What do you mean what going on with us?'

"Come on Lisa. I've known you long enough to know when something is up. You haven't called her to tell her where we are going for lunch, or that we are going for that matter!"

"Man, it's crazy with her right now. It's crazy with me right now."

"What do you mean by that?"

"Well, all we do is argue. It's like she blames me for all her problems. She has that review coming up with that Bishop Jones on Monday and she is all stressed out about it. She's taking it out on me like it's my fault."

"That's not new. She always gets mad at you when people don't approve of you two. You should be used to that by now."

"Yeah but it's different this time."

"How so?"

"This time I feel like it is. I can't stop feeling like if I wasn't a part of her life she'd be living a holy sanctified life like she talks about all the time."

"Wow! A holy sanctified life huh? What does that mean?"

"You know, like normal Christians live."

"Normal Christians?"

"Yeah, like your perfect little Ni."

"Don't go there. I told you she's not perfect and you know she's not."

"Yeah but you know what I mean. There is something different about us than you two."

"Not in sin there isn't. It's no different before the eyes of God that we made love outside of marriage than that you two do it."

"Yeah but all the crying afterwards and all that...that makes it way different. If she went through all that she was really sorry for what she did."

"Repentance. Yeah, that makes all the difference before God. You're right. So what are you going to do? You're not ready to give her up. She's not ready to give you up. Why feel guilty if you aren't willing to give up the sin?"

"I just don't get it. Why would God make me this way if it's not okay with him? My pastor claims it's fine with God but I just can't stop thinking about it. I wish I wasn't like this Josh." She broke into tears, "I really do wish I wasn't like this."

Joshua had never seen Lisa like this before. He had never heard her do anything except defend her right to be openly gay. That she not only felt but was willing to admit that she didn't want to be gay was something new. Joshua took her hand in his and spoke in a low voice, "Lisa, you don't have to be anything you don't want to be."

"Yes, I do. All my life I have wished I wasn't like this! When I was a little girl I hated the fact that I was so different! I tried to be like the other little girls and play with dolls and all that mess. I was just out of place. Then I would play with the boys and even though it felt more natural to play football and go craw fish catching I was still out of place! Why would God make me so that there is no place for me?"

"Lisa, none of us are born how we should end up. We all have things about us to shed and things about us to discover. Only fools stay the same all their lives. If you hate being gay why don't you ask God to help you be delivered from it?"

"What does that mean? To be delivered from it? I'm the it...it's me. I like women. I like the way they look, the way they smell, I like to kiss them, touch them, flirt with them, the whole nine! How can he deliver me from myself?"

"Well, I don't know how he does it. You know I'm not rcal religious. But I know there have been times when I have hated who I was and I asked Him to change me and He did. I don't know how. Some changes were easier to make than others. Some changes I asked for and when He proceeded to do the necessary work I decided it wasn't worth it. But I do know if anyone can change you, He can. All you have to do is ask."

"My Pastor said it's not possible. He said we are who we are from birth and that God doesn't hate us."

"Well, God doesn't hate you but he does hate sin.

Now you know I'm not religious but I do know God hates sin. If you are really ready to take a look at your life and make some changes it's not going to be easy."

A young woman came and placed a pizza on the table in front of them. Neither of them took any of it but both thanked her politely. Lisa wiped her face with a napkin and asked Joshua, "Can I ask you one question Joshua?"

"Sure."

"Do you think I'm going to hell?"

"How should I know? I have enough on my ands trying to make sure I don't end up there. After taking Benita to bed I'm sure I'm a little closer than I was a month ago!"

"How come you never tried to tell me that I was so messed up?"

"Lisa, come on. You're not all that messed up. Think about it, who was I when you met me?"

"You were messed up...bitter, sad, repressed,

anxious, you were like a time bomb!"

"Yeah, and that's just what you knew about. I was numb really. I couldn't feel anything. Nothing mattered, not even me."

"I remember. But you've come a long way."

"Yeah but I did it when I was ready. You never told me I was messed up to get me to change."

"I know but that is different. You were in pain, a little lost."

"Is it different Lisa?"

The two ate pizza in silence. Just before they finished it Joshua told her, "Really Lisa, if you want to change it's your choice. If you don't that's your choice too. We all have to live with the choices we make. I'll support you either way." He took a big bite of his last slice and said with is mouth full, "And let me know when you want to go dress shopping! I have been waiting for a long time to help you out in the fashion department."

"Help me out? I dress very well thank you!"

"You dress like a man and if you were a man you would not be considered well dressed. Sweats and baggy jeans does not qualify for well dressed."

"Whatever Mr. Metro-Sexual! Been to any good manicurists lately?"

"In fact I have. I was going to treat Ni to a day there. Maybe you two can go together."

As they were leaving Lisa's phone rang. It was Erin. As soon as Lisa picked up Erin started talking. "Okay Lisa I don't know what you are trying to do but I am already in enough trouble here at my job because of you and now you are trying to mess me up even more!"

Lisa asked, "Hold on...wait a minute! How am I messing you up? I'm chilling at lunch...and it's Saturday anyway. How can a Monday thru Friday job stress you out on Saturday?"

"You were supposed to take me to get a suit to wear for the review remember?"

Lisa had forgotten. She didn't think it was necessary for Erin to buy a new suit for a review with a group of people who had already hired her. In Lisa's mind it was a waste of time and energy especially if they were going to fire her. But Erin was convinced that she'd feel more confident in a new suit and added that it couldn't hurt to have a new suit if she was going to have to look for a new job.

"Oh E, I totally forgot! I'm so sorry. I'll be there in a few minutes. We're leaving the pizza place now."

"We? We who?"

"Me and Josh. Who else? It's Saturday. You know we do our thing on Saturday."

"Well forget it. I'm going alone." Erin hung up. She couldn't believe Lisa had forgotten all about her. Everything that was happening was so connected to Lisa and yet Lisa seemed so far removed from it all.

No matter how hard Erin tried to get Lisa to understand that the world was against them Lisa seemed to Erin not to care. It didn't matter to Lisa that people whispered and snickered when they went certain places. It didn't matter to Lisa that both of their families had groups of people who were practically starving themselves to death in hopes of the two of them breaking up. It didn't matter to Lisa that now Erin's job was in jeopardy and that her career might suffer greatly if her integrity was put on the line and found questionable or worse, to be nonexistent.

Lisa's response to all those issues was always the same "...It's not about them Erin. If we are going to be to together or if we are going to break up it's about us." Erin thought it was the most selfish mentality in the world to live life as if everything was about just her. If Erin lived that way she might have long ago left Lisa based on all she went through defending her right to be with her. But Erin understood that Lisa was counting on her to be true to what she had promised so long ago...that she would never leave her. They had agreed that any break-up would be a mutual agreement and not one person leaving the other high and dry. Both of them had experienced abandonment in the past and didn't want to be subject to it or subject anyone else to it.

Now that things were heating up in Erin's life as a result of her commitment to Lisa, Lisa seemed to be going along like everything was just as it should be. Erin had no idea of the internal struggle Lisa was facing.

While it was true that Lisa would not live her life to please any of the people who judged her, it was also true that Lisa wanted to live a good wholesome life. Up until recent months Lisa thought she was doing that. She was a good person. She regularly attended the Rainbow Church of the Savior and lived a life of giving, loving and being a good person for the most part. She was faithful to Erin. She was kind to strangers. She was very forgiving and she took to heart the lessons taught by her pastor every Sunday.

But a while back Pastor Mike had taught on the

adulteress whom Jesus had saved from stoning and Lisa had not been able to shake the lesson she had received that Pastor Mike had not imparted into her.

Pastor Mike focused on the fact that there were none who had not sinned, that there were none who had the right to accuse or condemn the woman. He commented that Jesus was the only one with that authority and that Jesus had excused the woman...set her free from her accusers.

But Lisa realized Jesus had set her free from more than her accusers. Jesus had set her free from her sin. He had saved her but it was not unconditional. His last words to the woman were "Now go and sin no more." Those last words were not a part of Pastor Mike's sermon but they were the most real part of the story to Lisa. She knew that if the woman had gone and revisited her sin she might not have received the same forgiveness the second time around.

When Lisa asked Pastor Mike about that aspect

of the story he assured her that Jesus would always forgive the woman as long as she asked with a sincere heart. But a heart sincerely wanting not to be stoned and one truly repentant for sin were two very different things to Lisa. She had spent her whole life coming to Jesus asking Him to keep people from stoning her. Now that the stones were flying more than ever before she wondered if it was time to examine her actions, her heart, her motive for coming to Him in the first place. Was she prepared to accept the charge to "Go and sin no more"?

After agreeing to meet up with Joshua later on at his place to throw some burgers on the grill Lisa got in her car and sat for a moment praying, "Lord, I know I am a sinner, I know I have offended you...that I always offend you. I also know you love me. I can't take all this chaos Lord. It's too much. I just want to live in peace. You are the Prince of Peace and I don't understand why I can't seem to touch in with that peace when I love you so much. I know I have been very judgmental to Christians in general. Forgive me for that. But what am I supposed to do? All my life I've been like this. I wouldn't know how to change if I wanted to."

Lisa heard a small voice inside her answer with a simple question, "Wilt thou be healed?" Lisa burst into tears.

Chapter Nine

Bishop Jones had asked Nikki to meet him at his house for an informal meeting to discuss the situation at the daycare center. She had never been to his home before and was a little nervous about going. He had told her to dress casual and to come with her hair let down so she wore a pair of capris and her favorite t-shirt. The outfit was simple but she had accessorized it to the hilt and looked like she was walking out of a modest music video. She laughed as she looked in the mirror and realized her version of casual took more time and accessories to put together than any other style she might wear.

She called Benita on her cell and asked her to pray. "Okay Ni. You started this mess so I need you to pray for me all day okay!"

"I didn't start no mess. But I will pray. Are you on your way over there now?"

"Yeah."

"But I thought the board meeting wasn't until Monday."

"Yeah, that's the official meeting with Erin. This is the pre-meeting where they sap me for info before they get to her."

"Oh right. Well, I'll pray but I ain't fasting today! My man is taking me some where special and I have a feeling it involves eating. He loves to take me to cool places to eat. Maybe he's trying to fatten me up so nobody else likes me."

"Hey, as long as he likes you it's cool right? Wait a minute...did you just call Joshua your man?"

"Yes. I did. We are official as of last night."

"Ooh la la! I'll have to get details later."

"There are none to get. He said so what's up, you my lady or what? And I said, yeah, I guess I can be your lady. So we kissed to make it official and that was that." Benita neglected to tell her friend that the lovemaking prior to his question had, for Benita, sealed the deal. She had not yet even told Nikki about the first time they made love weeks prior and she didn't know when or if she ever would. She couldn't stand the thought of Nikki lecturing her on being holy.

Benita knew all about holiness. But with Joshua she didn't feel dirty or sinful. She felt like a real woman in his arms. She had talked to The Lord about it and He had warned her that she could not hide her sin for long nor could she escape the consequences of her actions. She had not talked intimately with The Lord since then. She didn't want to know what those consequences were, not now while Joshua was still so exciting and satisfying. She knew God was well aware of her love for Him and that she would eventually find her way back to Him. But for now she was fully committed to enjoying her short reprieve from her chaste life.

"Listen Nik, Joshua is special. I really like him. I think I might be falling in love with him...I know I am."

"Duh! Just be careful Ni. What's done in the dark..."

"What are you saying? I can't fall in love?

Lisa had long ago told Nikki and Erin about Joshua and Benita's first night of unrestricted passion. Despite throwing hint after hint, nothing Nikki said clued Benita in on the fact that it was not as big a secret as Benita wished it was. "Never mind Ni. I have to go. Pray for me. I'll talk to you later"

Nikki went to her fridge and took a bottle of cold water with her and left her house. Bishop Jones lived almost 30 minutes away and she didn't want to have to try to find some where to get a drink on the way. She had been making sure to drink as much water as possible lately since she had watched a show on women's health and had learned that women needed to consume four times as much water as she typically took in each day.

She listened to Donnie McClurkin in the car which made the half hour drive short. She was not entirely ready to get out and end her worship experience when she arrived at Bishop Jones' home. As she pulled up she double checked the address. There were quite a few cars parked out front and she had not been informed that it was going to be a big social event. Sure that she was indeed in front of the correct house Nikki got out of her car and was happy to hear the same song she had just turned off blasting from the back of the house.

She walked up to the house and rang the doorbell and within a few seconds the Bishop's youngest daughter answered the door. She was soon to turn four and wasted no time telling Nikki so. She had barely opened the door when she started chatting, "I'm Deborah. People call me Debbie but I don't like it very much. Debbie is a little girls name and I'm almost four so I think you should call me Deborah." Bishop Jones' wife was close behind Deborah and greeted Nikki as she stepped into the beautiful home. "Nikki," she pulled Nikki in for a warm gentle hug, "It has been a while huh? I think we haven't spent time together since I was pregnant with Little Olan right?"

Bishop Jones and his wife had 10 kids. After giving birth to six daughters by way of a set of twins and 4 singles, the couple resorted to adoption in an attempt to gain a son. They had chosen to offer themselves as anti-abortion options for single young women. The local clinic ran a program through which women who were diagnosed to be pregnant and did not want to be could immediately go through a catalog of potential adoptive parents and begin the selection process right away. The adoptive parents would then support the young woman by providing health care and whatever else she might need to ensure a healthy baby and as comfortable as pregnancy as possible.

It turned out that all 3 times the Jones' had been chosen the women all had girls. At last Bishop Jones convinced his wife to try one more time for a son. A year later their only son was born. Bishop Jones was more than delighted to pass his name along at last...little Olan Jones the fourth was now almost 2 years old and Mrs. Jones was pregnant again, and just starting to show. The ultrasound had confirmed that another son was on the way.

"Oh wow!" Nikki smiled, "Number 11 in the oven huh?"

Mrs. Jones smiled, "Yeah. This little one took us by surprise. He must have a special assignment from The Lord because He had to sneak him in!"

The two women laughed together as Mrs. Jones led Nikki through the house to the back yard. Nikki was shocked to see the entire board of trustees in the yard as well as kids, teens and a few people she didn't know. She made her way around greeting people and being graciously received. Bishop Jones gave her a big bear hug as always. He was a tall ,wide, strong man who was loving and loud. "Nikki! You made it girl! I thought you had changed your mind."

Nikki asked, "Am I late? I'm sorry. I thought you told me 1:00."

"You know what, I did tell you 1:00. I told half the people 1:00 and half 12! At first I thought 1:00 and I called a bunch of you. Then I talked to Patty realizing I hadn't run it by her and she said to tell everyone 12. So everybody I called after that got 12. I didn't think to call the rest of you back and tell you 12. It slipped my mind."

Mrs. Jones smiled, "He likes to spring stuff on me when I least expect it." She rubbed her belly playfully and winked at Nikki, "This was supposed to be a few folks coming over to talk about the daycare center. Then he thought he may as well feed whoever showed up and of course that meant barbecue. Then he realized he couldn't have a barbecue and not tell the whole world about it!"

Bishop Jones smiled, "Aw come on now Patty, you know this ain't but a tiny bit of who I might have asked. Outside of the board there are only a few folks here...Nikki, did you meet my nephew over there...Linus. Linus! Come on over here boy!"

Nikki had not met Linus. She had no idea how she had managed to go around the whole yard greeting church mothers and saints and deacons and not lay eyes on him. He was gorgeous! For a brief moment Nikki wished she could be a fruit of the loom a-frame and conform her shape to nestle on his every distinguished upper body curves . His skin was perfectly dark chocolate, his physique was chiseled, is teeth were white as all things lovely and white and when he opened his mouth and responded to Bishop Jones Nikki could have passed out swooning in the deepness of his voice. "Hold on Unc. I'm captured over here!" Little Deborah had him painting her fingernails which was a compromise from her original request of him letting her paint his.

Bishop Jones laughed, "Oh man you better watch out! I was taking a nap the other day and woke up with pink toenails!" Everyone laughed as Nikki reminded herself that she was there on business not pleasure. She made a moderately hefty plate of food and sat down next to Mother Harris, the oldest member of the board, to eat. She had learned long ago not to play food shy with Bishop Jones. He was a man who loved few things more than cooking and sharing food with the people around him. He would say that people who struggled to stay stick skinny needed deliverance and would go to preaching on how much Jesus loved to feast.

Mother Harris wasted no time questioning Nikki. "What's going on over in that daycare center Nikki? I hear some strange things. I must say if what I hear is true I am disappointed that you haven't tried to contact any of us and make us aware of the situation."

Nikki had a mouth full of the best potato salad she had ever eaten. As she finished chewing it Bishop Jones put his hand on her shoulder, "Now mother, let the girl eat! We'll deal with all that in due time."

Nikki was relieved, not because she was not prepared to

answer any work related questions, but because she really wanted to fully focus on the delicious food on her plate.

Linus came and sat across the table from her with a modest plate of food. He announced as he got comfortable, "Round three! Ding Ding!" Several people laughed as Nikki tried hard not to seem too prissy eating but also trying to be ladylike as she dealt with the wonderfully messy barbecued beef ribs.

Linus watched Nikki unashamedly and asked, "Okay, now tell the truth. If this was your mamma's house and you were eating those ribs would you be using that napkin every five seconds or would you be licking your fingers?"

Nikki smiled, "Actually I'd still be using my napkin."

Linus announced, "Oh oh, we have a dignified saint in the house folks!" He smiled at her as Mother Harris defended Nikki, "Now you leave this young lady alone you trouble maker. She don't want to be all heathen like licking on her fingers and what not. That's for brutes like you."

Mrs. Jones sat down beside Linus with a piece of chicken in her hand, "And me!" She put the chicken down on her plate and sucked the sauce off her fingers requesting, "Bishop, will you bring me and Nikki a few napkins? In fact, bring those wipes over here and bring me one of those ribs....and a taste of potato salad…no, macaroni salad...no potato salad. In fact, put a dash of both on there and a little seafood salad too!" She winked at Nikki again.

Bishop Jones complained happily, "Woman, I may as well make you a whole plate! You and that boy eating up a storm today ain't you?"

"You know what honey, that's not a bad idea. Make me a plate like you made earlier only smaller portions and 86 the chicken. I have a piece."

Linus asked Nikki, "Do you have kids?"

"No. I've never been married."

Linus grinned, "Now lets not pretend never being married equals no kids these days. They are two separate questions. But thank you for answering both for me. That was next. So how old are you?"

Mother Harris interrupted, "Uh uh, no you don't. You don't ask a woman you don't know her age! Bishop...you tell that brother of yours this boy of his needs some training!"

Bishop Jones came and set his wife's plate in front of her and playfully whacked his nephew in the back of the head.

"Unc! What was that for?"

"I told you to go easy on her didn't I?"

Nikki was slightly uncomfortable knowing that there had been discussion about her prior to her arrival but the more she thought of it the better she felt. Bishop Jones must have anticipated some attraction or connection to have to prep his nephew. She didn't get the feeling there was any resistance in regards to it and that gave her a sense of security that overtook her initial discomfort.

She talked with Linus for a while after she finished her food and before Bishop Jones called her inside for the meeting. She had almost forgotten why she was there and excused herself from the relaxed and entertaining conversation she had been having with the man she internally referred to as "Dark Chocolate".

Chapter Ten

As Nikki walked aggressively to her car she fought back tears. How could they try to put the chaos going on at Sweet Blessings on her? Yes, it was true that she had been employed by the daycare center longer than anyone else and it was also true that she was a trusted member of the church of which the daycare was an outreach program . It was also true that she was probably the only person working there who might have felt comfortable calling any of the board members on the phone to report on what was happening.

But Nikki didn't understand how she had some how become the watchdog. No-one had consulted her when they hired Erin. She worked for Erin like the rest of the teachers and assistants and she did not assume her longevity with the center afforded her any additional responsibilities any more than it afforded her special privileges. Nikki worked as hard as anyone else with the same rules, regulations and responsibilities as the other lead teachers. Nothing more and nothing less.

Mother Harris had been adamant that Nikki had breeched some level of confidence, had broken some unsaid code by not making Erin's sexuality known to them . The rest of the board members, while not as obviously offended as Mother Haris, did agree with her.

Somehow Nikki's befriending Erin had become something that it wasn't. It was the general feeling that if Erin and Nikki were not such good friends Nikki would have long ago called some one and told them about her. Nikki could not convince anyone that she and Erin were not as close as it was being presented. They had gotten reports otherwise from the teachers and parents alike.

~   ~   ~   ~   ~   ~   ~   ~

Nikki dug through her purse searching for her keys frantically. She desperately needed to enter the safety of her car so she could let the tears loose. She dumped her purse on the hood of the car and did not find her keys in the contents. She remembered that Deborah had been carrying her purse around for a while and that it was likely that her keys were some where that Deborah had been playing.

The thought of going back inside to face everyone was not a welcome one to Nikki. She had nearly bolted to the door, not having said goodbye to Mrs. Jones or any of the other guests lingering in the yard. She didn't want anyone to see how upset she was and at this point she just knew the board members would be reporting on the meeting to everyone which meant they would all know how close she had come to tears.

"Lord help me please! I can't go back in there! I just can't!"

She turned and leaned her back against her car and slid down it. She sat on the ground and held the tears back trying to gain the strength to go back inside to find her keys. She took a deep breath and as she was about to stand up she was startled by a deep. newly familiar voice. "Nikki? Are you out here?"

It was Linus. He jingled her keys and gave a cat call, "Here Nikki, Nikki, Nikki, Nikki!"

Nikki stood up glad to be half smiling at his silliness. "I'm right here."

"What in the heck were you doing down there?"

"Never mind." She turned and faced him and was taken by his looks all over again. She bit her lip seductively and was instantly embarrassed that she had.

"Um, yeah, I was thinking the same thing about you." Linus was unashamed. "What in the heck happened in there? Everyone came out arguing and upset. What are you up to at that daycare center?"

Nikki was offended that he has assumed what she had been trying to convince everyone wasn't true. "I haven't been up to anything! Someone else's issues are somehow my responsibility and it's all a big mess and I'd just like to go home....please." She put her hand out for her keys. Linus considered tossing them to her but decided not to and walked towards her slowly.

The closer he got the faster her heart pound. By the time he was near enough to put the keys into her hand she thought he must have been able to hear her heart trying it's best to jump clear out of her chest. He put his hand out for her to take the keys as he asked, "Is it so bad? Do you really have to go?"

Nikki stared into his pleading eyes. He somehow seemed more vulnerable in that moment than she felt. She reached for her keys and as she would have grabbed them he swiped his hand away and smiled, "Not so fast cowgirl. I asked you a question."

The vulnerability Nikki had gotten a glimpse of was gone and all that she could see was the ornery, testing flicker she was so used to seeing in the eyes of her 3 year old students at the center. " I really should go. It's complicated."

"No. It's simple. I have your keys and you didn't say goodbye to my Auntie who is searching around looking for you declaring that she just knows you wouldn't have left without doing so."

"Ugh!" Nikki rolled her eyes, "Really? Is she really looking for me?"

"Yeah, she really is. She likes you a lot. So does Unc. You are all they talked about last night when I got here. Well, you and the choir."

"Oh, the poor choir."

"Yeah. The poor choir."

(The choir director had gone off and gotten married and moved to Texas and now the choir was in a mess trying to elect the new director. The most capable person was not the most popular and the most popular was totally inept when it came to directing. So the two alternated weeks directing and the result was not harmonious to say the least.)

Linus opened his hand with the keys inside, "Here, take em. Go. Leave me here with a million kids and old people. It's cool. It's not like we're old friends or anything...who am I right? What's it to you that I'll be bored and have to endure Unc teasing me that you ran away as fast as you could?"

"Oh Lord have mercy! If I ran away from anyone it was Mother Harris!" Nikki snatched her keys suddenly, embarrassed that he didn't try to swipe them away. They both smiled and he asked once again, "Come on, do you really have to go?"

Nikki smiled and admitted, "No, but if I do stay my ego is going to have to wait for me here at the car."

Linus extended an arm of gentility to her, "Don't worry, I still have mine with me and it's big enough to cover the both of us!"

Nikki smiled and linked her arm in his. They laughed and walked back together. They walked around the house through the side yard and admired the many rose bushes along the walkway. When they reached the back yard an applause broke out. Everyone welcomed Nikki back and congratulated Linus on a job well done.

Bishop Jones slapped his nephew on the back, "I didn't think you could do it boy! She was hotter than this smoking grill when she went out that door! I'm glad though. Business is business Nikki. What goes down in the office has nothing to do with what happens out here in the yard! Now sit on down next to Mother Harris and you two kiss and make up!"

Nikki was strangely not embarrassed at all the attention and obediently sat down next to Mother Harris who took her in her arms and squeezed her tight. Nikki could not prevent the tears that burst forth from her and Mother Harris comforted her, "Now cut that out Little Miss. We all love you around here. If we are tough on you it's because we know what The Lord put in you and we want to make sure it gets out. You don't go around living a mediocre life when you are called to be extraordinary."

Nikki's sobs quickly subsided and Mrs. Jones handed her a wipe to clean her face. She was glad she had opted to go au nturale. Linus exclaimed, "Hold on now, you mean to tell me you aren't wearing make-up?"

Nikki blushed. Mother Harris stated, "There you go again! She's a natural beauty son. You can't buy that kind of beauty in the stores or at the plastic surgeon's office!"

Nikki spent the rest of the afternoon enjoying the family like atmosphere and everything about Linus. He teased her constantly but not in a way that was hurtful. He made just enough fun of her to let her know he was paying attention to her even when she thought he wasn't.

As afternoon tiptoed into evening Nikki knew she needed to get going. Many of the guests had already left and Nikki did not want to overstay her welcome. She made her way around to everyone saying "See you tomorrow in church" and when she got to Mrs. Jones she thanked her profusely for her hospitality.

"Oh Nikki. You know you are special to me. I

don't see enough of you. If I had it my way you'd be here every weekend with us. One way or another we end up feeding someone every Saturday. Usually we pay the Kittlings' to do all the work for us. Their catering business is struggling lately and we sure don't mind resting. But they were out of town this weekend so honey had to get on the grill himself."

Nikki rubbed her stomach and stated, "Well, I for one am glad he did. Those ribs were out of this world!"

"Oh yeah, those Jones men can burn. Honey can bake, grill, fry, whatever. He's a better cook than I am!"

NIkki whispered, "That's what I'm talking about...a man that can preach The Word and fry up some chicken!" The two women high-fived and laughed as Linus approached behind Nikki. Mrs Jones stated, "I didn't get the last of the Jones men Nikki. There's one right behind you that I hear has a few talents of his own."

Linus pretended to be embarrassed, "Auntie,

please..."

She continued as if his plea had not been uttered, "I'm surprised he didn't mention it to you... Linus just got his pilot's license. That's his latest hobby. He's an architect by trade and he can cook his butt off too. He can't dress worth nothing but I guess you can't win em all can you?"

"What's wrong with how I dress? It's Saturday!"

"Saturday or no, that is an undershirt. Am I not correct Nikki?"

Nikki didn't know how to respond. She was very much in favor of Linus wearing a frame shirts every day of his life with the upper body he was sporting. But she understood the old school mentality about undershirts not being shirts. Her mother would have had the same complaint, "Well, I think that is a generational issue. It's like slips, women these days don't really wear slips like they used to when I was growing up."

Mrs. Jones chuckled, "Oh when you were

growing up huh? Way back then?"

Nikki was a little embarrassed and Linus saved her, "Okay Auntie, she needs to get going...you and your half hour goodbye over here. It's not like you won't see her tomorrow in church!"

Mrs. Jones hugged Nikki tight and whispered in her ear, "He'll be in town for a week...maybe you can convince him to stay."

Nikki smiled and blushed. Linus asked, "Uh oh, what did she just say about me? Man, around here you just never know what's going on!"

Nikki made a gesture as if to zip her lips and turned to leave the back yard. Linus followed her to her car where he stepped awkwardly close to her, "So," Nikki backed up and he smiled, "I'm not going to bite you. I just wanted to get a last whiff of you. I'm a strange kind of guy. I love the way a woman smells when her perfume combines with her natural smells."

Nikki was mortified! Was he trying to tell her it

was time for a shower? Was that why he had rushed her away from Mrs. Jones?

He went on, "It's not a bad smell at all, just a special sweetness. That end of the day female smell...it drives me wild."

Nikki folded her arms close against herself and Linus laughed, "No really...you don't stink! You smell great. In fact, if I am not mistaken you are wearing one of my favorites...Sanctified Passion right?"

Nikki was a little impressed but still held her arms close to her body, "Yeah. I wear it all the time. It's my favorite. That and Blue Hymn."

"Oh so you're a Kingdom Personals product line fan huh?"

"Oh absolutely. Kingdom and Mary Kay all the way. I gotta support the Godly businesses."

"You remind me of my mother. Kingdom and Mary Kay...those are her brands. Just tell me you don't put ice in your milk when you drink it."

"Of course I do..if it's not cold enough."

Linus rolled his eyes, "No way! But it dilutes it and makes it all watery...yuck!"

"Not if you drink it fast enough. You don't sip on a glass of milk Linus. It's not like a glass of wine"

Linus stepped close again staring searchingly into Nikki's eyes, "Mom? Is that you in there? How'd you fit in that little body?"

Nikki pushed him away playfully and he sniffed hard and winked. Nikki put her arms back in folded defense position and tried not to smile.

"So Nikki...I'm in town for a week or so. I know you have a lot going on with the daycare center in turmoil and all but do you think we can get together some time?"

"I think we could. What brought you to town? Vacation?"

"No. I just sold my business up north. I got tired of it. I've been in the business for so long. I started working in construction when I was in 8th grade and I did it all through high school and college. I got my degrees and opened my own construction company, built this and that...schools, little shops, modest homes, million dollar homes, churches, you name it. I'm just not into it anymore. I've lost the creativity, the fire, the excitement of it all."

"Oh. So now what...fly planes?"

"No way! I do that for fun. I couldn't do it for a living. I don't know what's next. Unc wants me to stay here and take some time to figure it out. Of course he wants me to direct the choir in the meantime."

"Oh really? You?"

"Yeah. Heck yeah. Now that still excites me. When you got a few good folks, that's all it takes is a few voices... and they really want to give God The Glory....Man!" Nikki was surprised by the excitement that he showed. She would not have guessed this about him.

"Well," Nikki admitted, "If we ever needed you we need you now! Our choir is a mess, really. They wont follow the directors because there is all this political mess about who the director should be. Half of them sing the songs how the old director taught them despite the fact that the interim directors have shown them new ways to sing them, half of them won't sing at all but stand there pouting...it's a mess!"

"I know. Unc told me all about it. He said he might suspend all of them until he knows what to do. He said the Praise and Worship team is still on point though."

"Yeah, they don't care who leads, who directs, they just love to make a joyful noise you know? But the choir, that's a whole other story."

"Well I know what I would do with them. I'd disband the choir and make everyone audition again..."

"...again? Nobody auditioned in the first place. If you want to sing show up for rehearsal and after 3 consecutive rehearsals you can sing on Sunday."

"That's problem number one. I'd audition people and in the interview process I'd ask questions about why they want to be on the choir. You'd be surprised how honest people will be when you flat out ask and they haven't had time to manufacture a response. I'd only accept the people who answered that they just want to be a blessing. That's all there is to it."

"Sounds simple but that would offend a lot of people."

"Jesus offended a lot of people and He still does. We are commanded not to be easily offended. Jesus never said to be un-offensive. If they are offended, they'll just have to pray."

"Wow. You're a little militant deep down inside huh?"

"When it comes to things of The Lord I don't play games. Ministry, no matter whether it's singing on the choir or handing out backpacks to needy kids, whatever it is, if it's done with The Lord's name attached, it must be done in the right spirit. Otherwise people get the wrong impression of The Lord and we're held accountable to that."

The two stood in silence for a moment before Linus spoke again, "So, when can I see you again? Or should I say will you see me again? I know I just got all deep on you. I know that can be a turn off."

Nikki was anything but turned off by his stern approach to ministry. She smiled and as she opened her car door instructed him, "Get with me after church tomorrow. We'll figure some thing out then." As she got in the car he answered, "Okay, so dinner after second service it is."

"I didn't say that."

"You didn't have to. See you tomorrow."

Chapter Eleven

Erin and Lisa sat in the front row of the Rainbow Church of The Savior. They had been members for several years and had never sat in the front row before. Erin was uncomfortable but Lisa was determined to sit up front with or without Erin. Erin, who had seen many woman at the church checking Lisa out over the years, was not going to let anyone get the impression that they were no longer together. She followed Lisa to the front row and settled in.

As the Pastor spoke on Jesus' encounter with the woman at the well Lisa became agitated. She noticed how he managed to preach the same message he always preached. He spoke about how Jesus didn't spend time condemning the woman for her sin but that He simply loved her.. Lisa knew there was some thing missing from his sermon. She knew that this woman would not have gone back to her old lifestyle. If she had how would the entire town have been transformed? What was to transform if everyone continued in their former state? How could this man stand in front of all these people and mislead them? Lisa's head was spinning. She wanted to stand up and yell, "It's not true! We're all going to hell! We must repent! We must turn from this wickedness!"

Instead she stood up and passed out.

A short while later she awoke with a crowd of people standing around her and Pastor Mike telling her to relax, "We've called the medics, they are on the way. You'll be fine."

Lisa tried to get up but Pastor Mike and Erin pushed her back to the floor. Erin was harsh, "He said relax Lisa! Don't try getting up! You just had a seizure! Just relax!"

"A seizure? I don't have seizures! Let me up. I'm

fine. I just got a little light headed."

Pastor Mike spoke with a firm hand on Lisa's chest holding her down, "We don't know what just happened. You stood up and mumbled something and then started shaking and hit the floor. It was very strange. Just try to relax and the medics will be here soon okay."

Lisa was thoroughly confused. She had never had any medical problems at all. She was always strong and healthy. But her head did hurt and she did feel like she was in a dream world of some kind with all the people standing around her. She asked if it was alright if she at least sat up and Pastor MIke and Erin both frowned and shook their heads. Lisa closed her eyes and resolved. She would stay in place until the medics came.

Meanwhile at True Gospel Church of the Trinity Benita and Nikki stood in amazement. The choir which had squawked and screeched just a week prior was standing in front of them harmoniously bringing forth song. Before them stood Linus with arms gracefully and authoritatively directing them. Bishop Jones had called the choir members after Nikki had gone home and asked if they wanted to hold a short rehearsal with his nephew and within a half an hour all but two of the members were in Bishop Jones' house obediently submitting to the direction of Linus. In two and a half hours they had reworked one of the former director's signature songs in such a way that most of the members of the church were on their feet or in tears or both.

The excellence of Jesus was celebrated through the simplicity of the lyrics and the intricate arrangement of the harmonies. Nikki would not have told anyone what she was experiencing. Between wonderful rushes of worship and adoration of her savior she experienced moments of pride in Linus that she had no explanation for. She had only met the man less than 24 hours prior but as he stood ministering before her she wanted him to be long to her and vice versa so badly that she was almost ashamed of herself. She had never mixed a worship experience with longing for a man before and she was not sure if it was sinful or not. All she knew was the more she admired him the more she admired The Lord for having created such a magnificent man. She contemplated man's being created in God's image in a whole new way and wondered if Linus' movement at all resembled the Lord's conducting the universe.

Tears streamed down her face and as she looked to her friend beside her she was crying too. Benita's tears were sorrowful tears as she finally admitted to herself that no matter how much satisfaction she was getting from Joshua it was sin to be having sex with him. As the choir rang forth the words "Every knee shall bow and every tongue confess..." Lisa sobbed. She had betrayed her one true love and she did not know how he would ever forgive her. More to the point she did not know how she would ever forgive herself.

~   ~   ~   ~   ~   ~   ~   ~

Joshua sat on the small deck in back of his house. It was quiet and he stared at the book on the table in front of him. It was his wife's Bible. He remembered how she read it every night before she went to bed. She never forced him to listen or to read it. When she did go to church, which was seldom, she never forced him to go with her. Every now and then she would mention Jesus when she humbled herself after a fight and she told all the Bible stories to the kids. Other than that religion had not been a major part of their lives.

Joshua ran his finger over the words "Holy Bible". He talked to God out loud, "Okay, so I know you are real. We don't have to have that talk. And I know Jesus is the savior of the world and all that. I have no qualms about that. We had that talk a long time ago. And I know I haven't been to church in a while. But I haven't changed my mind about You. I am still saved, aren't I?"

He flipped through the pages of The Bible for a moment and then shut it again. " I still feel saved. But what's the deal with love? How are we supposed to know when it's right, when it's wrong? How can love be sinful? You said to love people? Look at poor Lisa...she's a mess! All because of who she loves. And you know I really like Benita. Okay, the truth is I think I love her. Okay, the real truth is I know I love her. She's amazing! I mean, really, you did a good job on her. I never thought a woman would impress me like my Lorena. Well, she's your Lorena now...I guess she always was really. Anyway, why does it have to be so hard just to love people and live life?

"Poor Benita hates herself for making love to me! I know it. And it's crazy because I know you sent her to me. I know you did. I was so lonely inside. Outside I was fine...but some nights...well you know. And the way she touches me! I know there's love in that touch. It heals some thing in me Lord.

"How can you use her to heal me like that and at the same time call it sin? How can it be a sin to love someone? That's all we are doing right?" He waited a while for a response and flipped the bible open again. He read the first thing that caught his eye..."But if anyone should cause one of these little ones to stumble it would be better for that man if a large millstone were tied to his neck and he was cast into the sea."

Joshua smirked, "Don't waste any time being subtle or anything...Right... subtlety is the other guys strategy, I know. So what are you saying? I can't be with her? I have to leave her alone? That's not fair!" He slammed The Bible shut and banged his fists on the table "That's not fair Lord! Why would you send her to me and take her away?" Joshua sat in silence. He was angry enough to cry but tears had long ago abandoned him. He sat with his fists clenched. "Can't I just love her Lord? Can't she just love me? What's wrong with that?"

In his heart he knew what was wrong with it. He

knew that love without honor was not love but a warped version of love. He knew that he was taking something from Benita that he was neither prepared to keep nor could he ever give back to her. He slammed his fists down on the table again and yelled "Fuck! It's not fair! I'm not ready for all that! I don't' even know her!" He knew he was now trying to justify what was unjustifiable. It was either true that he loved her or it was true that he didn't know her. He knew that both could not be true and that he would have to decide which one was and which one wasn't. He sat there fighting with himself for a long time.

Nearly and hour later he got up. He had come to a resolution that he would not tempt her again or cause her to sin with him. He was not prepared to marry her or even to contemplate marrying her. There were still too many unexplored territories with her. He had no idea how she was with kids, how she would be with his parents, how she was with her finances, how she kept her house when company was not expected. He knew all those things about Lorena long before they were old enough to even get married.

He decided that it was more true that he did not know Benita than that he might love her. He was not convinced that this was actually true but there was less chance of getting hurt or really hurting her to go with that option. He also knew that there was no way he was going to be able to date Benita and not want to touch her intimately. He knew he would want to make love to her when they were alone, that he would want to kiss her and hold her close. He knew that they had both already proven that restraint was not something either of them were prepared to exhibit.

Joshua banged his fists on the table and shouted "This is not fair Lord! This is not fair!" He would break it off with Benita when she came over after church.

~   ~   ~   ~   ~   ~   ~

    In the ambulance Lisa explained that she felt fine except for a slight headache as Erin rattled on and on with the same details about what had happened, "She was mumbling and she stood up and mumbled out loud and then started to shake a little and then fell down and was shaking like a mild seizure or something. Then she was still and opened her eyes. That was it."

    The paramedics kept trying to get Erin to talk less and Lisa to be more specific about what she had experienced but it was a futile attempt. At the hospital Lisa was very unhappy. Her blood pressure was high which it had never been and her vision seemed to be blurred slightly. When she moved her head suddenly the headache was worse and all she wanted was to go home and lie down. The doctor came in and explained that they would be keeping her for a little while until they could answer some questions.

Lisa was not at all interested in being a little while in the hospital no mater what a little while meant to this doctor. She almost barked at him, "A little while? What does that mean? A few minutes? Hours?"

"No. A few days. The tests we'd like to run will take a few days to come back and we think it is wise if we keep you here in the meantime just to be safe."

"What? No way! You have to be kidding! I passed out that's all... a simple head rush! I need to drink some water and go lie down which I promise I will do as soon as I get home." Lisa started to get up and Erin yelled at her, "Lisa! Chill! Listen to the doctor! If nothing is wrong they will know in a few days, but if some thing is wrong they need to know that so they can do what ever they have to do to fix it! Stop being so childish!"

Lisa was sobered by Erin's rebuke. She sat back and asked, "Okay, so what are we talking about here? What's so scary?"

The doctor explained, "Well, the mumbling combined with the irrational behavior...standing up suddenly...and then passing out, they are not typical symptoms for a simple head rush as you put it. I've noticed you seem to be having some trouble with your eyes too...correct?"

"Well, yeah, it's like I can't focus right away when I look from one thing to another. And the headache is worse when I turn my head." Lisa turned her head to the side slowly, "Not like this," she turned back more suddenly and winced putting her hands on her head, "but like that."

The doctor handed her a clipboard with a small stack of papers on it. "You'll want to look over these before signing. The nurse will be in in a moment to go over any questions you may have."

Lisa was starting to feel afraid and asked, "Doctor,"

"Yes," he listened to her heart for a moment and

then looked to her for the rest of her question.

"What are you thinking is wrong with me?"

"Well, to be honest, it could be any number of things. It is too early to tell without having run very many conclusive tests."

"Yeah I know but what are we talking, dehydration or stress type of situation or brain cancer or aneurysm type of situation?"

The doctor looked at Erin who was standing with her arms folded and a very stern look on her face. Then he answered, "I can tell you that it is not dehydration. Stress can be related to a number of more serious problems. I don't like the irrational behavior. I can tell you that. But without running the proper tests we can't say. Lets just wait and see what comes of the tests before we get excited okay?"

He turned and left the two women alone. Lisa stared at the light above her and Erin moved close to her and put her hand on Lisa's. Lisa jerked her hand away and asked, "Can I just have a minute E? I don't do well with sickness, you know that. This is a lot to take in. Give me a minute."

Erin was hurt and hissed, "You know what, have all the time in the world. I'm going home. Call me when you can think about someone besides yourself." She picked her purse up and as she was leaving she stated, "You're not the only one who is afraid right now Lisa. I had to watch you shaking and sputtering like a fool. People are going to want to know why I'm not here with you...like it matters." She walked out and cried her way to the lobby where Pastor Mike was waiting. She dried her face with her sleeve when she saw him and he came up to her anxiously,

"How is she? What are they saying?"

"They are going to keep her and run some tests. I'm going home. Can you give me a lift?"

"Yeah, sure. Of course. But don't you think you aught to stay with her?"

"No Pastor. I think I aught not."

Chapter Twelve

As service let out Nikki and Benita stood near the doorway of the restroom waiting in line. Benita's mood was as sober as Nikki's was jubilant. Nikki whispered to Benita, "Didn't I tell you he was fine? Oh Lord! And he looked even better in that suit! No, that's a lie...he looked pretty delicious in that A-frame yesterday."

"Yeah, Nik. He's handsome. Your type."

"Honey he's a whole lot of women's type...he's fine! And anointed too! Umph! He had that choir on point! I wonder when they rehearsed. He just got in on Friday and he didn't mention that he had rehearsed with them when we talked."

"I don't know. Maybe last night after you left."

A female choir member who was standing in line behind then informed them, "We rehearsed last night. And he is fine isn't he? I got to get moving! I'm not about to miss my lunch date with that fine thing! My divorce is almost final too! Oh yeah...it's on."

Nikki was shocked and overruling her better judgment which would have waited for more freely given info she asked, "Oh so are you two dating?"

The woman sneered, "Girl. Me and Linus go way back. He used to come here every summer and stay with Bishop. And every summer it was on!" She did a swervy dance and continued, "I haven't seen him in years but as soon as we laid eyes on each other we both knew it was on again! I'm looking forward to this lunch date, I'll tell you that!"

Nikki's heart sunk into the pit of her stomach. She should have known he was too good to be true. It didn't make sense for a man that fine not to have a wife anyway. She should have figured he was a player. She turned to Benita and asked, "How bad do you have to go? This line is so long, we could be home by the time we get in there anyway."

Benita knew her friend just wanted to get away

from the woman who had just burst her bubble, "Girl, lets go. I just wanted to freshen up a little anyway but I can do that back at your place. I still have some time to kill before I meet up with Joshua." They left and rode back to Nikki's place in relative silence.

At Nikki's they brewed fresh mint tea and Benita broke the quiet mood with a question, "Nik, you aren't thinking about standing him up are you?"

"You know I am. Why?"

"You don't know what him and that woman have going on. You know women lie all the time to try to stake claim on a man they want. You've done it before and so have I. I say you give the guy a chance before you toss him back in the sea."

"I don't know about that Ni. Why should I waste my time on a player? I might miss the real blessing running after some nut."

"I'm not saying you should run after him. Just don't stand him up. He'll only be in town a week you said right?"

"Right."

"Well, see what he's about and if he's a loser you won't see him after next week anyway. If not, well who knows what might happen."

Nikki sipped her tea and looked at Benita questionably, "You're unusually open minded. What's up with you? Are you okay?"

"I just know I've been really hard on people lately...well all my life really. It's just because I try so hard to be perfect. Then I think everybody else is supposed to be perfect too. But I'm not and no-one else is either."

"I've been trying to tell you that for years."

"I know. But Joshua said some thing the other night that really hit me hard and I can't stop thinking about it."

"What did he say?"

"He said that Jesus didn't have as high a standard

as I do and that if Jesus who was perfect could forgive people for all their sins, murder, rape, all of it, who did I think I was to hold little things against people ... especially myself."

"Wow. That's true Ni. I didn't think Joshua was very religious though."

"He's not. He was raised a Christian but he's not into it all like that. His wife was more than him. He just tries to be a good guy but he doesn't do the church thing and all that. He is saved though."

"Well he sure ministered to you huh?"

"Did he ever. In fact, I better go. I'm meeting him for lunch and we have a lot to talk about. You take a short nap and go on back to second service like you always do. Then go out with that man and have some fun. You don't have to elope or anything. Just have dinner and laugh."

"I don't know Ni."

"Girl, just go. Promise me you'll go."

"Fine. I'll go. Call me later."

Benita went into the powder room and freshened up before heading out to her car. As she got in she asked The Lord for strength. She was determined to tell Joshua that she could not make love to him again and if he wasn't prepared to date her in a more acceptable manner before The Lord they would simply have to stop seeing one another.

When she got to Joshua's house he was sitting on the steps in front of his house. He looked sad and Benita wasn't sure it would be a good time to have a deep relationship talk. She sat down next to him and asked, "What's up Josh? You look like the world is on your shoulders today."

"Yeah, it kind of is."

"Well, you want to talk about it or should I let you have your space? Do we need to reschedule?"

"No Ni. It's us. We need to talk."

Benita was afraid of what was to come. She had

intended to draw a pretty hard line but she was not prepared to have one drawn for her. "Yeah, we do need to talk. I actually had something I wanted..."

"Look, I really like you Benita. In fact I'd go so far as to say I've fallen in love with you. I don't know how it happened so fast..."

Benita was both thrilled to hear him say he was in love with her but confused by the fact that he couldn't look at her. He stood up, "Lets go inside," he said reaching to help her up. Inside they went into the kitchen and stood awkwardly close. Joshua offered her something to drink and she refused. His gaze kept falling on the floor between them. She took his chin gently in her hand and lifted it. He looked into her eyes and she saw a very alarming amount of pain and confusion in him. "Josh, I'm really not feeling very secure right now so whatever it is just come right out and say it okay."

"Nita," He dropped his gaze again, "I just think this is moving too fast."

Benita played with her purse strap nervously, "Yeah I agree. I was going to say the same thing. I think..."

"Look, I can't be your husband. I know I should have thought of that before we made love. I'm so sorry. But I'm just not ready for that. It's different with you."

"I'm not ready to be your wife either Josh. But what's different? What are you talking about?"

"The other night when I asked you to be my lady...what did that look like to you?"

"Look like? I don't know. I guess more of what we had already started, just more official...exclusive."

"Yeah, well we can't do that Benita. You are a woman of God. You belong to God and I'm out of line to be putting you in the position I put you in."

"We have both been way out of line. That's what I wanted to talk to you about. I think we shouldn't make love anymore. If we can't date without the sex, maybe we should..." Joshua cut her off with a deep passionate kiss. She melted in his arms and found comfort in the truth of the love she felt as he pulled her close to him. Everything about the way he handled her told her he was not lying when he had said that he loved her. Her touch and reception of him spoke the same to him.

Benita's breathing became a heavy pant and she burned with a desire for him to move the thin layer of fabric that kept his hand from touching her flesh. She grabbed his hand from around her waste and lifting her skirt placed it on her thigh. His hand against her bare skin took her breath away and she let out a quiet little groan. Suddenly Joshua pulled away from her and looked into her eyes with an expression that was unyielding.

"We can't even have this conversation without wanting to make love Benita. Do you really think we can date steadily...or even every now and then...and manage not to give in?"

Benita's head was still swimming with passion

and she was not sure how to process being so abruptly left standing alone. She frowned and shook her head slightly, stepping close to him, "Josh, don't say that. We can try." She put her hand on his chest and stroked it softly. He took her hand in his and lifted if to his lips kissing it gently. Looking her in her eyes he managed to say what he did not think he was capable of saying to a woman he loved so intensely, "I think you should go."

"What?" Benita snatched her hand from him and ran it through her hair, "Just like that?"

"Let's be real Benita. Which one of us can resist the other?"

Benita stepped back and tried to convince him that she could resist him, "I can do it Joshua, if I set my mind to it. I managed to stay celibate for years! Plenty of guys tried me in that time but I knew how to resist. I think I can handle..." He stepped close enough to her to kiss her and spoke softly, "You can do what Benita?" His lips were so close that as he spoke they brushed against hers, "What is it you can do?"

Benita's eyes were closed in anticipation of the kiss she desperately wanted but he did not kiss her. He simply asked again, "Tell me Benita, what can you do?"

Benita would have spoken if she could have. She wanted to say "I can resist you!" But what she did was lean into him and take the kiss she had been waiting for him to give to her. It was a sweet kiss, full of passion, love and fear of loss. Too soon for Benita Joshua stepped back and said, "I am asking you, please, will you just go?"

Benita knew he was right. She knew she would always want to taste his lips and feel his touch against her flesh. She knew she would always want him to know her deep inside where she was vulnerable and soft. She knew her desire for him was only rivaled by her respect for him now that he had done what she never would have been able to do. But her respect for him was far less than the rage she felt at being rejected by the man who she had given up years of chastity for. She turned furiously and moved quickly to the door hoping with everything inside her that he came running after her. She got to the door and struggled to open it.

He did not come.

She flung it wide banging it against the wall and bolting out.

He did not come.

She flew to her car and fumbled in her purse for her keys.

He did not come and as she looked up at his house she did not see him staring sadly out the window. She did not see him regretfully pining for her to turn back. She got in her car and sped off in tears.

Joshua stood in his kitchen and cried out "Why Lord? Why can't I just have her?" He fell to his knees and begged "Lord, please, it's not fair. It's just not fair. I love her. I swear I do. You know I do. You made me love her. Why would you make me hurt her like that?"

A small voice inside him reminded him that he had not been told that he could not have her. He had only been told that he could not cause her to sin. Joshua was the one who had decided it was more than he could handle to honor her as it was fitting to do.

When he understood that, he did some thing he had not done since two police officers had shown up on his door many years ago. He clenched his fists and as if to pull his frustration from his body, drew his hands to his stomach and he cried. He was bent over and broken. The tears flowed out of him with the sobs of resignation. He did not know if he was ready but he knew that he was not ready to lose the only woman he had loved since Lorena. But he had seen the fury in her eyes as she left and he felt her longing for him to follow her.

Joshua knew Benita was not a woman particularly practiced in forgiveness. He could not imagine what he could do to ever convince her to even look at him again. He had no idea what he could do to get her to talk to him, or listen to him, or even think about him without getting angry. She was a woman with a very cruel anger but he knew that he would have to face it, defeat it, and win her back. He would never forgive himself if he did not at least try to take things slow with her and see if they could build something positive together.

He pulled himself together and went into his living room and dropped himself down on the couch. On the coffee table his phone sat blinking. He picked it up and saw that Erin had called him five times. He called her back and as she told the details of what had happened to Lisa he made his way to the hospital quickly.

Chapter Thirteen

Nikki entered the center whistling. Her date with Linus the night before had gone so well she had almost forgotten about the drama unfolding at work. He had taken her to a nearby carnival where they spent the evening like two high school kids, running, eating soft pretzels and sweets, winning and losing at simple games and being whirled around on rides that reminded both of them of their childhoods. When the sun went down and the lights came on Nikki and Linus slowed their wild running about to a leisurely stroll. They didn't talk about much of importance. They simply let the hours pass enjoying the comfortable simple connection between them.

Linus was a perfect gentleman. He made no moves to get physical with Nikki except when they tussled playfully for the last of the cotton candy. When he dropped her off at the church to get her car he didn't try to kiss her despite the fact that they both knew a kiss had been begging to be shared all day. Linus gave Nikki a modest hug and sent her on her way home with a smile on her face.

Nikki was glad she had followed Benita's advice. She had not had such an unassuming date in a very long time and whether or not Linus was a player, he had managed to treat her with nothing but respect.

Less than 12 hours later she was putting her code into the keypad at work trying to push Linus to the back of her mind, and Erin and all that was going on at the center to the front. As she entered the building she walked into the midst of a group of the teachers gathered outside of the office. Erin was seated at her desk and was having a very loud conversation on the phone, "Well sir I don't know what to tell you. All I know is only four kids are here today. Yes, I did hear the rumor about a boycott but I don't know much about it. Yes I am sure someone around here has heard more about it. Yes, I'll find out what I can sir. Yes sir. Any preferences on who to send home? Okay. Yes sir. Oh yes, I will be there tonight. Okay then Goodbye."

The teachers scattered to get away from the office door as Erin got up and came to the door and opened it, "Look, you weren't all just passing by the office. I'm not stupid." The teachers meandered their way back towards Erin who spoke curtly to them, "This is the situation, The Bishop wants to know if anyone knows who is organizing this boycott." The teachers all looked around in silence. Erin continued, "Nobody has anything to say? Two of you have already talked to me a bit about it and I know the rest of you have more info than you are sharing. Integrity ladies, come on." Still no-one spoke up. "Well then you can all go home except for you Nikki. The Bishop said to keep you here. You can do what you can with the few kids that are here. It's just the Middleton crew and Baby Nancy."

The other teachers complained about hours being short and Nikki having favor with Erin. Erin cut it short, "The Bishop said anyone who valued their job enough to talk could stay but that the church was not going to pay anyone to be a part of any conspiracy. So if you still want to play stupid like you don't know who is doing this it's your choice. There are lots of people out there looking for work."

One of the teachers snickered, "Yeah, you'll be out there with them soon." Erin spoke angrily, "Who said that? Cowards. Go home all of you. Nikki, set up in the infant room. It's easier than dragging all that bay equipment to your room. In fact just go relieve Betsy and I'll bring you some stuff to do with the Middleton kids."

Nikki obeyed without question. The situation was far worse than she imagined. When she entered the infant room she found Miss Betsy comfortably seated in a rocking chair with baby Nancy in one arm and Taylar, the youngest of the Middleton kids on the opposite knee.

"Hey Miss Betsy. You can go on home. I'll be staying I guess."

"Well that's fine by me! All three of them Middleton kids got green mess coming out of their noses This poor little baby don't stand a chance!" Nikki wondered why Miss Betsy was holding a sick child and a well infant at the same time but she didn't make a fuss about it. As Miss Betsy put Taylar down she wailed before her feet hit the floor. Miss Betsy handed Nancy to Nikki and said, "I think Taylar has a fever. She's been stuck to me like glue all morning. They all need to go home if you ask me."

Nikki knew it would not go over well with the Bishop to be sending 3 of the 4 kids who had shown up home but she also knew their policy on fevers and infectious colds was not one they played with. "Miss Betsy, will you let Erin know when you get out there so she can decide on what to do please?"

"Sure thing. I guess I'll see you tomorrow."

Miss Betsy left Nikki alone with Nancy who was trying to fall asleep, Taylar who was face down in the floor wailing and Brian and Kevin, the Middleton boys banging trucks together. Nikki was more tired of her job in that moment than she had ever been. She asked, "Lord, is this really my life? I thought I would travel the world and be an evangelist. How did I end up stuck here with sick kids and drama and suspicion?"

Erin came in with the cordless phone in her hand. "Betsy says the Middletons are sick. I'm looking at them now…. Yeah, green snot and fevers. Ok. Will do." Erin hung up and exclaimed, "Great! What next?"

Just as she asked the question her cell phone rang in her pocket. She sat the cordless phone down on a nearby shelf and retrieved her cell phone from her pocket. It was the hospital and she quickly answered, "Hello? Lisa?…Oh, yeah this is Erin. What? Next of kin? Oh my God, what's happening? A coma? Oh my Lord. Yes. Yes. I'll be there as soon as I can get there." Erin hung up and sat down in the rocking chair next to Nikkki with her head in her hands.

"Erin what's going on?"

"It's Lisa. She's in the hospital and she just slipped into a coma." Nikki was shocked and sympathetic, "Oh sweetie, I'm so sorry, what happened? You need to get over there! Call Bishop Jones and let him know what's going on. I can surely handle these three."

"You know what Nikki, I really don't need you telling me what to do! Damned Lisa! Why does she have to do all this now? I'm holding onto this job by the skin of my teeth...she probably did this on purpose!"

Nikki asked in a sarcastic tone, "On purpose? Who goes into a coma on purpose? Listen, Bishop Jones will understand. I'm not trying to tell you what to do but I think you should call him."

"You just want me to seal the coffin. I'm not stupid. Now when the center is struggling I'm too busy with my girlfriend to be here right? I'll tell you who I'm going to call...Mrs Middleton. She needs to come and get there three before they give SARS to this little baby here and I'll be here when she gets here. As for Lisa, she'll just have to wait unit later. I mean, what is she going to do? Get up and leave before I get there? She won't even know I'm there if I do run over there! This is not a time for emotional responses. This is a time to be level headed and calm and that's what I am going to do." Erin grabbed the cordless phone and left the room.

Nikki could not believe what had just happened so rather than dwell on it she decided to do what she could to bring some peace to the atmosphere. She put Nancy in her favorite swing and picked up Taylar whose wailing stopped as soon as Nikki touched her. She cleaned Taylar's face and sanitized her hands. Then she put a soothing worship CD into the player and cleaned the boys' faces. She took the trucks from them and handed them soft blocks, sitting down with sanitizing wipes to disinfect the trucks. She rocked and talked to Taylar, "Okay little Momma, you are burning up. Lets take your temp okay?"

Taylar had a fever of 101.9 and her brothers both had fevers of 101.1. "Well, I guess you guys do need to go home, or to the doctors better yet. So lets just chill for a little while Taylar. I'll tell you all about my date last night. I went to the carnival! Do you like carnivals?" Taylar paid Nikki no mind at all but concentrated hard on putting the block she was holding in her mouth. Nikki went on about her date and was quite relaxed when Erin burst in the door, "You can go home too Nikki. Mrs. Middleton is on her way and I'll sit here with Nancy. I already passed it by the Bishop. He said it's fine."

Nikki was happy to get out of the madhouse that the center had become. It was strange to her that such an empty place could be so full of chaos. She stopped by the mall on her way home and as she was sitting in the food court she saw Linus come in the door. He was followed by the woman who had spoken of him in the line of the restroom at church. Nikki had accepted his explanation that the two simply made a date to catch up since they had not seen one another in so long but now she wondered how stupid he must have thought she was to have bought it so easily. She watched them walk to the counter of the salad cafe'. She contemplated hiding so as not to be seen or walking up to them and making her presence known.

Her pride wanted her to see Linus in extreme discomfort but The Holy Spirit told her to be still. Nikki followed the leading of the Holy Spirit and sat watching from afar. The two ordered and waited for their salads and left together. Nikki wondered why they had come to the mall just for salad but she was determined not to ask. In fact she decided then not to talk to Linus again for any reason.

She looked at her watch. Benita would still be up for another hour. Nikki called her and asked if she could come over. Benita was glad for the company as she had been fighting depression all night and the battle was most fierce now that she was home from work, tired, and lonely. For weeks she had been calling Joshua and talking to him while she settled down and got ready for bed. Now that she wasn't talking to him those hours before sleep were long and saddening. Not only was Benita fighting depression but she seemed to be fighting some flu. She was nauseaus and irritable and thought Nikki might distract her from how bad she felt with the details of the unfolding drama at the daycare center.

As Nikki left the mall she noticed Linus standing alone. As she focused more intently on him she noticed he was dialing his cell phone. Her own phone buzzed in her purse and when she took it out she saw that he was calling her. She ignored the call and walked to her car hoping he hadn't seen her. A moment later she received a text from him which stated that he was at the mall and that he was thinking of her, wondering if it was too soon or inappropriate to buy her something. Nikki erased the text and drove to Benita's house trying her very hardest not to be excited about what Linus might buy her at the mall. When she did not answer his text Linus got in his car and decided not to make a fool of himself. He told himself, "If she wants to talk to you, she knows the number bud. You had a fun night last night. If she's interested she'll get the message and call. Otherwise, et it go."

~   ~   ~   ~   ~   ~   ~

At the hospital Lisa was having a very strange dream. She dreamed that she was floating in mid air with a tunnel leading up above her and one leading down. She noticed that the door below her was dark and frightening while the door above her was full of light and very inviting. She thought, "This must be heaven and hell."

At that moment the door to hell swung wide open

and she felt herself being pulled towards it. She yelled "No wait! Wait!" But there was no strength in her to resist the pull downward. Quite near the doorway from which screams and every terrifying sound and feeling poured she yelled with every ounce of herself, "Oh Jesus! Please save me! Help Me!"

With that the pull downward stopped moving her and she floated as if suspended. She heard a voice ask "Do you know me?"

She cried, "Lord, Jesus, is it you? Yes. Yes I know you. I know you."

The voice asked, "Do you love me?"

Lisa cried, "Yes. Yes I swear I do. I love you."

She remembered the words she had read so many times "... if you love me keep my commandments". She sobbed and begged, "Lord I do! I try. You know I try. But it's hard! I don't know how to!"

The voice spoke to her again, "You have not asked me."

Lisa began to strive to get higher and though she made no progress she gained strength in striving, "Lord, show me! Please, help me! Please save me! Save me!" Lisa began to fly upward in a motion much like swimming. As she did she felt layers peel away from her. It was painful but not unbearable and the relief was beautiful as each layer was removed. Memories came to her and were drawn away with each layer that was removed. Lisa was very close to the door of light now and she felt love and peace and a great desire to see it swing open so that she might be pulled through it into the joy and rest that lay beyond. But in an instant Lisa was gone from the door, back in the hospital room where she could hear everything going on around her.

She could hear her mother crying and praying. She could hear the slow beeping of machines. She could hear the hiss of the air conditioner. She wanted to open her eyes but could not. She lay there pleading with God to take her back to the door and please let her in but there was no kind voice speaking to her now. Lisa exhausted herself and drifted back into sleep, dreamless and deep.

Chapter Fourteen

Weeks had passed since Benita has spoken to
Joshua. She had called him twice but he had not
answered. The first time he was at the hospital visiting
Lisa and had his phone turned off. The second time he
had gone to church with his mom and it was turned off
then as well. He had no idea that she had even called.
Now, as she sat on her toilet holding a positive
pregnancy test in her hand she wanted nothing more than
to talk to him but now more than ever her anger towards
him raged within her. Not only had he seduced her, not
only had he abandoned her, but now she was left to carry
the weight and shame of their sin alone. She would be
sat down from the auxiliaries she served on at church.
She would be the biggest joke of the year at the hospital
where she worked. After all her preaching and going on
about fornicators there was no way she would be left
alone in peace now that the fornicator was her. Nikki

was sure to be ashamed of her and there was no telling how her parents might react.

She was angry with Joshua for causing all this sin her life but she was more angry that she could not call him to come and hold her hand in this pivotal moment of her life. She had always been so hard on women who had chosen abortion but now that she held in her hand a positive pregnancy test she considered it. She more than considered it. She was almost certain it was the only way out of her shame. Surely The Lord could understand that she was not prepared to love the child of her lust. How could she? If she gave birth to this baby all she would ever think of would be how it had ruined her life, her good name. Surely The Lord knew she was not one who had an easy time forgiving. How could she be expected to love this...this...child.

"Yes," she said to herself, "It is a child. It is the child of sin, your sin. Now what will you do with it? Will you nurse it to health and adore it? No. You know you won't." She cried and resolved to get rid of it before anyone found out about it. If she was going to have to live with her sin for the rest of her life she was not going to take it out on her child. And she wasn't going to let other people have the joy of throwing her sin up in her face either. When she would decide to have children they would be the product of love, a stable holy environment, not some whimsical fling with some random guy.

But Joshua was not some random guy. Even though Benita was angry with him and still very hurt by him she knew that if he showed up on her door in that very moment she would put all that to the side and fall into his arms. She threw the pregnancy test in the trash with force and stood up. She was too ashamed to look in the mirror as she pulled her pants up. She washed her face quickly before leaving the bathroom. The way she figured she had about eight weeks to schedule and appointment.

She spoke into the air, "Okay Joshua, you have 6

weeks to show up here and tell me everything is going to be alright or I'm going to get rid of this baby. I can't do it alone. I cant carry and raise a baby by myself. I can't and I won't. Lord forgive me but I just cant."

~   ~   ~   ~   ~   ~   ~   ~

Nikki had been working for Joshua since the board decided to let her go. At first she was very angry but Mrs. Jones had come to her and prayed with her for an understanding heart and The Lord had given her one. It was not like Nikki had been the only person to get fired. The board decided to close the center for the summer and revamp it in the spring. The boycott had gone on for two whole weeks and Bishop Jones had gotten many anonymous letters demanding that the lesbian be fired. He was disappointed with the parents but only a few of them were willing to be reasonable. They had decided that Erin was evil and that Nikki was also for being her friend.

There had been a story in the local paper about the whole fiasco and Bishop Jones was not one to play games with the reputation of the church. With only a few kids still attending anyway it was the board's decision to shut down and start with a fresh new director and a fresh new approach in the fall.

Erin had filed a lawsuit against the church for firing her. She spent her days at the hospital fighting and arguing with Lisa's family members over what rights she should be afforded. As the weeks passed Erin's visits to the hospital became more of a ritual than a real desire to be with Lisa. She would sit and stare at Lisa with contempt. If she didn't think people would say that she was untrue she would have stopped coming after the first week.

She and Lisa had not been doing well prior to Lisa's incident. She knew it was irrational but somewhere inside her she did feel that Lisa had done all this on purpose. She knew Lisa could tell she was wanting out of the relationship and didn't know how to get out without breaking her promise. She knew that Lisa could feel her growing distant and mistrustful. Erin had actually planned to break up with Lisa if the board had suggested it but it was never offered as an option. They had simply let her go on the premise that she had withheld information about her lifestyle from them in her original interview.

Technically that wasn't true and Erin was hoping to find a lawyer who would agree. She had been through two lawyers who had both suggested that Lisa's irate moments at the daycare weighed more heavily than any of Erin's complaints about unfairness.

She sat beside the window in Lisa's hospital room wondering what she was going to do with herself all summer. Her unemployment would sustain her but she knew she could not sit and do nothing for months on end. As she pondered, Lisa's mom came in the door. "Oh Erin. I didn't know you were here. I thought you come later on Saturdays." Lisa's mom put a fresh bouquet of flowers on the nightstand and removed the old ones from the vase beside Lisa's bed. Erin snapped, "It's Friday. I always come in the mornings on Fridays. That was our agreement was it not?"

Lisa's mom was mildly apologetic, "Oh yes, it is Friday. I'm sorry." She rinsed the vase in the bathroom and took a bottle of spring water from her large purse filling the vase with it. "Well, I'm here now. I hope it's not a problem but I'm not going to drive all the way home now that I'm here. Have you eaten breakfast? I'm hungry. I was going to stop and pick up something but I forgot I was hungry when I was at the florists. No wonder she thought I was nuts! I asked her about the Saturday special and when she said she didn't know I gave her quite a look! I thought she was just trying to get a few extra dollars from me!" She laughed at herself and asked again, "Are you hungry?" She put the fresh flowers in the vase and smiled at the beauty of them. "I think I'll run and get something from one of those little shops nearby. What's the one you told us about, with the fresh danish?"

"Maddie's. It's right down the street. Go left out the main doors and you'll find it."

"I think I will. Can I bring you some thing back?"

"No....thank you." Lisa was not happy to have her alone time interrupted. She knew Lisa's mom was likely to make small talk with her all day. She looked at Lisa as the two werc left alone again, "Well Lis, your annoying mother is here and I get the feeling she'll be here all day. That means it's Bible time! Oh yeah, and don't forget the olive oil baths and the religious TV shows! Woo hoo what a fun day this will be! Maybe I'll go and let her have you to herself. Oh, no, some of the folks from the aerobics class are coming today. They'll be wondering why I'm not here if I go...dangit!"

~   ~   ~   ~   ~   ~   ~

Nikki sat on Joshua's desk swinging her feet. "Okay, so are you going to call her today?" She had been trying to convince Joshua to call Benita and vice versa but neither of them had done her bidding. Nikki had a feeling Benita was pregnant but she didn't feel it was her place to mention it to Joshua without proof. She knew Benita would be furious for her suggesting that she had fornicated if she mentioned it to her so she just prayed and tried to get the two estranged lovers back together. "Come on Joshua...how long are you two going to pout? It's been weeks! If I can get over losing my job you two can get over whatever you're getting over."

"It's not that simple Nikki. It's not some thing to get over. I just have to know how to approach her. I really hurt her and you know your friend, She is vicious."

"Yeah well I know she tried to call you twice so she must be ready to talk about whatever it is."

"You keep saying she tried to call me but I never missed a call from her or got any message."

"I know she tried to call you! Come on, call her!"

Joshua had come up with lots of elaborate plans for how to get Benita back but he had not gotten up the courage to try any of them. The plans were all great but what was he going to say to her if she did take him back? Wouldn't they still have the same problem? And there was no way she was going to want to hear him pop some weak proposal after he had rejected her. He knew whatever he did was going to have to be special, and as of yet he had not come up with anything that even impressed him greatly.

"Listen Nik, I love Nita. But I can't control myself when I'm with her. She's like a magnet. I just can't keep my hands off of her, or my lips, or any part of me! You have no idea what she does to me!"

"I am sanctified but I'm not a virgin. I know all about the passion bug. Once you taste of it's fruit...

well...it's hard not to want it. I understand. But you two can work it out. When I'm with her she just pouts. Now I have to see you everyday and you're pouting too! It's miserable. What did you do so horrible?"

"She didn't tell you what happened?"

"No. I imagine it had some thing to do with sex. That's the one thing she wont talk to me about. She has no idea I know you two did it. I tried to hint to her that I know so she'll open up and talk about whatever went down but she just wont. I think she's..." Nikki stopped herself.

"You think she's what?"

"Crazy. Stubborn."

"Yeah. She is. I love that about her. She's like a pit bull...relentless."

"I don't think you want to compare her to a pit bull when you call her." They laughed and Joshua looked at his watch. Nikki took the hint, Her ten minute break was over and she needed to get back to her class and relieve Marisol, her co-teacher. Nikki liked working at this center but she was glad she was only filling in for a teacher on maternity leave. Nikki didn't like caring for children in a secular way. She had been warned not to share her religious beliefs with the children so as not to offend any of the parents. This often put Nikki at a loss for words when little ones wanted explanations that required the truth of, "Because God loves us and he doesn't want us to hurt ourselves or each other." "Because I said so and I'm the boss" was a very sorry substitute.

Nikki wanted to tell Bible stories to the kids at nap time. She wanted to pray over their boo boos.

She walked back to her classroom and felt her phone vibrate in her pocket. She read the text that had been sent. It was from Bishop Jones and it said simply "last chance, he leaves tomorrow". Nikki had assumed that Linus had made himself at home in Miami. He had stayed for over a month. He had been working with the choir and had been involved in the men's ministry. She had heard a rumor at church that he was "taken" and she hadn't asked for details about whom had "taken" him. She figured he and his old flame had gotten back together now that her divorce might be final.

She peeked in on Marisol and asked, "Can I take another minute to make a quick phone call?" Marisol was reading a book to the children and nodded pleasantly. Nikki dialed Bishop Jones' number. He picked right up. "Hey little lady! How have you been?"

"Fine Bishop."

"Hey I want to tell you I'm real proud of how you handled that situation at Sweet Blessings. Folks were betting you'd leave the church if we let you go."

"Really? Well, I guess most people would, or at least some people. I'm fine though. I'm working with a friend for now...it's a temporary position but it keeps me busy."

"Well good for you! Is it teaching?'

"Yeah, three year olds."

"Good for you! Listen Nikki, my wife had me contact you. She told me to get you over here for dinner tonight or she'll have my head."

" Bishop, I'm not sure..."

"Listen, I don't miss much. I saw what that woman was doing to you at church, trying to make it look like her and Joshua had something going on. She's the reason he stayed away so long. She hounds him. Now they have a lot to work out but it's not like she wants you to think it is."

"Bishop, I don't think that's my business..."

"Listen young lady, I see the way you watch him. And I see the way he watches you. Everybody does. Now I don't know what happened between you but I know my wife wont leave me alone until I promise you'll be here for dinner tonight. You young people can work it out on your own after that."

"Bishop...I..."

"I know, you'll be here. 6:00." Nikki heard Mrs Jones yell in the background, "5:00!" Bishop Jones corrected himself, "Oh 5:00. I'm sorry. Can you get off work that early?"

"Yeah. I get off at 3:00."

"Okay. See you at 5:00."

"Yes sir." Nikki felt like she had just gotten off the phone with her dad. She smiled. It was comforting to know Bishop Jones and his wife were still in her corner. It was also comforting to know they weren't afraid to boss and bully her into doing what she had to do to win in life. She ran into the office to tell Joshua what had just happened. He was happy for her and teased her about talking so much trash about how she didn't care who Linus ran around with.

Nikki called Benita to tell her the news but when Benita answered she sounded weak. "Ni? You okay?"

"No. Well, yeah, I will be. What's up?" Benita had been throwing up all morning and had not been able to get to sleep. She had not gotten decent sleep in weeks and had been trying to change her shift hoping that might help but she had not been able to convince her supervisor to make the change.

Nikki was concerned, "You sound bad Ni. What's going on?"

"Nothing. I'm just tired. What's up?"

Nikki told her about her conversation with Bishop Jones. Benita was happy for her but could not bring herself to get excited. She had just called the clinic and scheduled an appointment for the abortion. She didn't see the point in suffering for another two weeks when she knew she was going to get rid of the baby. It seemed like prolonging it was just more torture. Benita wanted to get rid of the baby and move on with her life.

She tried to show enthusiasm, "Nik. I'm really happy for you. I am. I'm just really tired. Call me and let me know how it goes. I'm off tonight."

"I thought you had to work until Sunday?"

"I did but I called off. I need to get some rest."

Nikki knew something was very wrong. Benita was not the type to call off especially with such short notice. "Benita, what's wrong?"

"Nothing. I'm sure I'll feel fine tomorrow. Just call me later and let me know how it goes with Linus." Benita hung up and Nikki stood wondering what to do for a moment. She turned and walked back into the office and said to Joshua, "Josh, something is very wrong with Benita."

"What do you mean?"

"I don't know. She sounds really bad though. She called off work tonight and she says she'll feel better tomorrow. I think she's pregnant Josh."

Joshua dropped the order forms he had been holding. "You think she's what?"

"I think she's pregnant. She' getting weaker and weaker and sicker and sicker. She's either pregnant or she's really sick. I think she's pregnant."

Joshua couldn't help the smile that overcame him, "Pregnant? By me? I mean, of course by me... I didn't mean that like it sounded...I mean, really Nik?"

Nikki was touched to see the joy in his eyes, "Well, I don't know for sure. But I think so. She hasn't said anything to me about it. She has no idea I know..."

"Oh wow! Pregnant!" He stood up and clapped his hands "Hot dog! Pregnant!" Then he frowned and said in a low voice, "Oh. I bet she doesn't think this is so exciting. Oh poor thing. She must be feeling so alone! How could I not have known? I knew when Lorena was. I knew the instant it happened. I don't know how I knew but I did. Oh wow! I can't believe it! Pregnant!"

"Well I'm not sure Joshua. Don't go buying cigars just yet. You might want to call her and find out."

Joshua looked at Nikki suspiciously. He wondered if she was just trying to get him to call Benita now that she was about to be re-united with Linus. "I'll call her Nik. I'll call her tonight and see if she'll let me come visit her. I promise. You said she called off work right?"

"Yeah."

"Okay, so I give you my word. I'll call her when I get off work."

The rest of the day passed quickly. Benita's appointment was set for 4:00. It was 3:30 and she was just getting out of the shower. She threw a sun dress on and left the house. She got in the car and drove to the clinic. She was sweating and nervous so she drove around the block once. She was still not ready to go in and drove around once more. As she reached the parking lot the third time she parked and sobbed. She sobbed for almost an hour and hadn't noticed the time.

Inside the clinic Evelyn Johnson looked over the appointment list and noticed Benita's name on it. She looked around and saw that she wasn't there yet. She also noticed that Benita's name had been highlighted in red. That red stripe over her name meant that it was imperative that Benita have her abortion within the next 2 weeks before she reached the 4 month mark. Evelyn figured she'd get a hold of Benita and find out of she was on her way. But There was no phone number with Benita's name. Evelyn remembered that she had Nikki's cell phone number in her phone. She dialed the number and Nikki answered more so because she was curious about why she would be getting a private number than anything.

"Hello?"

"Hello, Um Nikki. This is Evelyn...Johnson."

Nikki was not happy to hear Evelyn's voice, she had been in the center of the drama that unfolded at Sweet Blessings. Nikki took a moment to remember that she was to be forgiving and asked, "Yes, Evelyn, what can I do for you?"

"Well, I know this is awkward but I'm actually looking for Benita. Would you have her number?"

Remembering where Evelyn worked it suddenly

occurred to Nikki why Evelyn might be calling Benita and she responded, "Of course I have her number, why is everything okay?"

"Yeah, everything is fine. I just didn't want her to miss her appointment. It says it's urgent so I just wanted to make sure she got in here."

The clinic director walked over to Evelyn and snatched the appointment book out of her hands saying, "Did you just call for Benita?"

"Yes, I have her friend on the line."

"Well, I don't see a number here for her! How did you get a number for her?"

"I know her. I know her best friend."

"You called her friend?" The director hung up on Nikki and told Evelyn off for putting patient confidentiality in jeopardy. By the time the two finished arguing Evelyn no longer had a job. She gathered her things and left out the back door.

In her car she cried out to The Lord, "Thank you

Lord!" Evelyn ad been working at the clinic for years. She started working there with the hope of talking women out of having abortions but she soon learned that it was company policy to talk them into them. She was disappointed but couldn't afford to be out of work so she had stayed. When she discovered that she earned a commission on each abortion performed that she had scheduled she was very torn. But the money was very good and most of her patients didn't need much convincing. After a while she justified it by reasoning that someone would get the commission so it may as well be her, a tithe paying Christian who would at least pray for the women's souls.

But since the unexpected pregnancy that had brought forth her twins Evelyn had an even harder time working at the clinic. She knew that unexpected blessings were often the best kind as the twins were more fun than anything and considering the work that they were it was a whole lot of fun! Still, as much as it had burdened her more each day to go to the clinic and assist in offering abortions; she needed the money more since having the twins than she had before. She knew she was caught in a trap but had no idea how to get out of it.

As she sat in her car she rejoiced at finally being free from the trap she had been in for so long.

Evelyn drove home and celebrated her new freedom over a bowl of corn flakes in chocolate milk...the one meal she craved more than anything when she was pregnant with the twins.

Benita drove around and around the clinic and called her mom telling her the whole story through sobs and tears. Her mother's simple response was, "Baby, come on home. Leave it all and just come home. I'll send daddy down to take care of that house. You can always find another job. You come on up here and have that baby and you don't have to worry about who thinks what. I dare anybody around here to have anything to say! You come on home."

Benita agreed and drove straight to her house. She packed a suitcase and grabbed a few pictures off the walls. Through sobs and tears she packed her car full of miscellaneous odds and ends. She tucked her house key under the mat and got in her car.

~   ~   ~   ~   ~   ~   ~   ~

Nikki called Linus and apologized for not being able to attend his farewell dinner. She explained that she had not been able to reach Benita and gave a few details about the situation without telling too much of her friend's secret. She and Joshua drove first to the clinic. They barged into the clinic searching for Benita.

Joshua was so upset the clinic director called the police on him. He went from room to room desperately trying to stop Benita from having an abortion. He saw her name on the list and was overcome with grief. No one at the clinic would say if she had been there or not. When Nikki asked to speak to Evelyn she was informed that she was no longer "with" the clinic. Nikki kept trying to call Benita on the phone but got no answer. The two were frantic seeking Benita. They were worried and they were not going to relax until they knew she was alright.

Three hours and hundreds of dollars of fines later the two had not found her. Joshua was devastated and Nikki was sad beyond words. They drove to Benita's house and Nikki used her key to let herself in. When they saw the state of the house they knew Benita had gone away in a rush. They wondered where a thirty four year old woman fresh out of an abortion operation might run to? Nikki tried to recall any place Benita had even mentioned wanting to live or even visit but Benita was a homebody. She did not long to see far off lands or even nearby states for that matter! Nikki called Linus and explained the whole story to him and he told her that he understood although Nikki knew he was disappointed that he would not see her before he left.

"Listen Nikki, you don't owe me any long explanations. We barely know each other. I'm leaving tomorrow. I'll check you out when I get back in town. I have a long day tomorrow. You take care."

Nikki was too tired and worried about Benita to put up much of a fight. "Yeah, that's cool. Give me a call when you are back in town if you find time." As Nikki hung up she had no idea what to do with herself. She sat on her bed and turned on the TV. A commercial came on advertising a savings and loan program. The announcer stated, "Just come home".

Nikki realized she might just know where Benita had gone. She searched for Benita's mom's number in her phone and dialed it. Benita's mom answered and Nikki cried to her that she had no idea where Benita was. Benita's mom assured her that Benita was fine. "She's going through a lot right now honey. She's coming home for a while. If she wants to get in touch with you I am sure she will. But give her some time Nikki. She really is on the edge."

Nikki didn't know what Benita had told her mother. She didn't know if she had the abortion or not, if she had shared any of that with her mom or if she would be driving Benita away from the one safe place if she blew her cover. As much as she wanted to mention it she didn't. Se just left a message that she loved Benita and that she would miss her. Nikki let Josh know that Benita had gone home to her parents and that she would not take calls from them.

Joshua was devastated. He had missed his chance to win her back and it had caused him his unborn child. Depression threatened to reclaim him but Nikki made it clear that neither of them were going to let this crazy time convince them that life was not good. As hard as it was at first they fought to have fun despite the great losses they had suffered. Eventually though, they found that smiles were easier to come by and that they could still hope for restoration, They encouraged one another to stay positive and kept one another busy.

Chapter Fifteen

Nikki and Joshua had become great friends and she was sad to be spending her last day at the daycare center with him. She knew that they would still spend time together. They had been almost inseparable since Benita had left. Nikki missed Benita very much and so did Joshua but Benita still would not talk to either of them. Her father had come and moved her things out of her house and had paid an agency to oversee the property and find a tenant to live in it. He made sure to touch in with Nikki when he was in town conducting business to let her know Benita was doing well but he never mentioned the pregnancy. Nikki assumed that Benita had gotten rid of the baby before she had left and Joshua assumed the same.

As the two of them recalled the night they met over lunch Nikki became sad. Things were simple then. Nikki's life was orderly. She had a best friend named

Benita who was like a sister. She had a job where she could listen to worship music all day and she had no sad memories of a dark chocolate man by the name of Linus. Linus had called her several times but Nikki made sure not to show too much enthusiasm when he did call. She was determined not to become his next Miami lover like the choir woman had apparently been for so long.

Nikki cleaned up her mess in Joshua's office to head back to her classroom. Joshua's phone buzzed and he looked down at it and saw that it was the hospital. He told Nikki, "Hey, it's the hospital, hold on a sec." One of the things they had come to do together was spend time at the hospital chilling with Lisa. They were in agreement that she could probably hear them and they didn't want to leave her out of their growing friendship. Erin had stopped visiting Lisa long ago and both Joshua and Nikki wanted Lisa to know she was still an important part of their lives.

Joshua stood up and asked, "Lisa?"

Lisa answered in a chipper voice,"Yeah. It's me."

Joshua yelled in her ear, "Hallelujah! Nikki, it's Lisa! It's her! I'm talking to her on the phone! Holy Lord!"

Nikki praised The Lord . She had prayed much for Lisa, mostly for Joshua's sake. Joshua talked to Lisa for a while and learned that she had been awake for almost two days. She had come to right after he and Nikki left the last time they had visited her. According to Lisa she had been trying to wake up the whole time but she just couldn't. She had heard almost everything that had happened over the months and shared her gratitude for Joshua and Nikki's coming and having fun in the room with her.

The doctors still didn't know what caused her coma but she was recovering so nicely with no signs of permanent damage that they had all but given up on trying to find out. One of the brain specialists had said to Lisa's mother, "It is as if something supernatural shut her down and months later flipped a switch and turned her back on again." Lisa knew there was more truth to that than he knew.

That evening Joshua and Nikki went to visit Lisa and they were surprised at how refreshed and vibrant she looked. They laughed and rejoiced together until the nurses came and directed Nikki and Joshua to go home. By then it was an hour past visiting hours. Lisa stopped them before they left the room. "Guys, there is some thing I want to tell you before you go."

They both stopped and the nurse who had come to escort them out paused and nodded to Lisa who revealed her news, "I'm not gay anymore guys. I'm free. I'm totally free. It's gone. I don't know how it happened except I had this dream and God was stripping stuff off of me. He was talking to me and everything. I never saw him but I knew it was Jesus. I knew it was. That was so long ago. It seems like years. I wanted to wake up and tell everybody, especially my mom who kept praying for me to be delivered. All I know is a few times God talked to me and kept asking me if I loved Him. He always made me feel like he loved me, not like he was mad at me or anything. But he always asked me if I loved Him. When I would say yes he would remind me to keep His commandments. But it was like a gentle request, not all harsh.

"He didn't have to be harsh. He saved me from hell...literally. I was on my way to hell and He saved me! You guys have no idea how excited I am about life. I get a whole new start. I'm a whole new person!"

Joshua, Nikki and the nurse had made their way to the bed. Joshua and Nikki were now sitting on the bed and the nurse was standing next to them. The three women all had tears in their eyes and Joshua shared their sentiments although no tears fell.

Lisa was beaming. It was as if The Glory of The Lord shone brightly in her eyes and off of her skin. She spent the next week recovering in the hospital and was soon home where she received physical therapy. Joshua and Nikki helped her develop a style that was lady-like and sophisticated which her mother was more than happy to fund. They burned all Lisa's men's clothes and had a bonfire party one night. As they were sitting under the stars discussing what to do for Labor Day weekend Nikki's phone rang. She did not recognize the number but contrary to her habit she answered it.

Linus was on the other end. "Hey Nikki. It's Linus."

"Oh Linus..." Lisa and Joshua teased like high school kids making kissy faces and batting their eyelashes at Nikki. Nikki laughed and Linus asked, "Is it funny that I called?"

"Um, no. What's up? I haven't heard from you in a while...at least a couple of months."

"It hasn't been months Nikki. It's been about four weeks."

"Five, but who's counting?"

"Right. Well, I know you are busy with your life and all, Unc told me about your new friend...the one who came out of the coma. And I know the center is going to re-open soon. That's pretty awesome. I love when real miracles happen to people I know."

"Yeah, me too. But you don't know her."

"Actually I do."

"You do what?"

"I know her...Lisa"

"How do you know her?"

"From Unc's. I met her last week. She was by there for some thing with Auntie."

"Yeah, New Member's class. She missed one because she had to go out of town for something and First Lady Jones agreed to give her and Josh a make-up lesson."

"Yeah right. I like Joshua. He seems like a pretty cool dude."

"Yeah. He's alright. So what's up? Wait, when

did you meet him?"

"He picked Lisa up at the house. But never mind that. I was wondering if I can see you soon?"

"See me soon? Look Linus, I don't know what you have in mind for us but I'm not a long distance lover kind of girl. I mean, it's obvious we are attracted to one another and I don't think we'd be too good at being just friends. It's awkward."

"I agree. It is awkward. Have you ever thought of why it might be so awkward? I mean, we really don't know each other very much."

"Yeah, I know. It is strange. But never the less, I'm not into the here one minute gone the next thing. I don't want to end up like what's her name on the choir."

"Okay, that was a low blow."

"Yeah well truth hurts sometimes."

"I bet you wouldn't say that to my face."

"Whatever. Like I'm afraid of you. Listen, I have to go. I'm at a friend's house."

"I know where you are. You're sitting next to Lisa in her back yard smelling the sweet savor of men's clothing burn away."

"What? How do you know where I am?"

"Because I'm staring at you out Lisa's window. Her mom is trying to feed me as we speak."

Nikki turned around to see Linus in the kitchen window waving at her with a big grin on his face. She spoke into the phone, "Oh my goodness, what are you doing here?"

"We'll get to that. Can I come out and join the party or am I forbidden to come into your presence?"

"Um, yeah come on out."
Nikki raised her fist at Joshua and Lisa who were in hysterics..."You should have seen your face when you turned around!"

"Yeah," Lisa laughed so hard she had tears running down her face, "You turned white...not white like me but white like snow! That was classic!"

Linus strolled across the yard towards Nikki. She stood up and greeted him with a formal hug, "It's good to see you Linus."

"Oh sure it is! I've been all but begging you to see me since June!"

"Well, I..."

"Never mind. Why don't you tell me what you were saying about ending up like Katrina?"

"Like ending up like who?"
Linus chuckled a little watching Joshua and Lisa move in to get a better vantage point.

Nikki smirked, "Oh Katrina."

"Yeah, don't play like you don't know her name. You found out everything you could about her before I left. People talk Nikki. Especially church folk!"

"Yeah, I know. How do you think I know so much about you and Katrina?"

"What do you know about me and Katrina Nikki?'

"Well, I know you and her used to get it on every summer back in the day."

"Yeah, high school days. Do you have any idea how long ago that was? What else?"

"I know that somehow you are the reason she is getting divorced and that ain't high school days. That's current."

Linus sat down and pulled Nikki's hand gently to sit down with him. She reached to pull a chair close to his but he playfully snatched her onto his lap. She tried lazily to get up but he said, "Oh no, you're going to sit right here until we get this straight. Then if you want to run away that's fine."

Nikki was happliy resolved to stay put as Linus told her how he had caused Katrina's near divorce. "Katrina's oldest daughter is not her husband's. She's mine."

Nikki tried to get up but he gently pulled her close again, "Wait. Let me finish. No-one knew that until last year. Brandi, her, um… our daughter, had some blood work done and her dad, um step dad, just happened to look over the paperwork and noticed that their blood types didn't match. It was crazy. After all these years for it to hit the fan like that. He was furious of course. Katrina was embarrassed. It was all a big mess.

"I didn't find out about it until the day after you and I met! She asked me to go to lunch and I told her no but Unc insisted. He said I needed to hear what she had to say. He knew the deal. In fact he suspected it all the time. He used to say her daught...um Brandi walks like me and laughs like me. At any rate...we were coming from getting the paternity test the day you saw us at the mall..."

Nikki was embarrassed, "You saw me that day?"

"Of course I saw you! Why do you think I called you and texted you? I was staring right at you when we ordered salads. I was wondering if you would come and say 'hi' but I guess that's not your style."

"I started to but...well never mind."

"Yeah well, I was going to come back in and sit with you but by the time she got in her car you were already outside. I was going to tell you the whole story then but you dissed me! I mean you dissed me hard too! And I was going to buy you ice-cream and an "I love Jesus" sticker that day! There is a vending machine there with these huge glittery stickers1 They're cool!"

"I know about the sticker machine Linus. I work with kids. Anybody who knows anybody under 10 years old knows about the sticker machine. But that's irrelevant. The truth is it didn't look good Linus… you and her, and all that stuff she was talking."

"Yeah, I am sure it didn't. But you have to be wise. Think about it...would my uncle...the Bishop... and his wife...your sweetheart First Lady Jones set you up with a guy who was going to dog you out?"

"Well, I didn't think of it like that."

246

"I know you didn't. You were so mistrustful of them because of all that mess with the daycare center..."

"Yeah, I guess so. I'm so sorry."

"It's cool. I'm a patient man. When Unc told me about you...all fifty hundred times...I knew you had to be special. And when Auntie had nothing but good things to say about you I knew you were very special. So I figured I'd wait around until you were ready for me."

"You've been waiting all this time for me?"

"Of course! I got a job flying planes so I could be available to settle down wherever and whenever you were ready."

"No way!"

"No... not really. I got a job flying planes because I was bored and I can fly all over the world for free!"

Nikki smiled. Linus smiled too and asked in a deep pleading tone, "I know it's a bit sudden but I've been wanting to ask you this since our date so long ago."

Nikki grew tense. She had no idea what was

coming next but she didn't feel prepared, "Um, go ahead I guess."

Linus smiled irresistibly and asked, "Can I please have a kiss? I've waited months for one and that's the truth."

Joshua and Lisa and the few friends who had tuned in to the whole conversation cheered as the two shared a gentle and respectful kiss.

Joshua's heart longed for Benita. He sent a prayer up to heaven for her well being and took a sip of his beer.

Chapter Sixteen

Linus and Joshua argued in the mall over whose suit was more GQ. They were being auctioned off at church for a fund raiser and they, along with thirteen other single men, had been instructed to have formal wear, work clothes and something they would wear to a family function for auction night. The Ladies Department had organized the event and were running it much like a beauty pageant. The bidding would be silent and the men were available for four chaperoned hours of service to the highest bidders and all proceeds were going to fund a needy family's Christmas.

After many weeks of preparation the event was finally going to take place. As the two men strolled the mall asking strangers whose suit was the most GQ Linus' phone jingled in his pocket. It was Nikki and she asked if he was alone. Linus answered, "If you call being in a crowded mall with Joshua alone I guess I am!"

"Shh!"

Linus excused himself from Joshua and walked away whispering, "Okay, I'm more alone than I was a second ago. What's up?"

Nikki shared some good news about Benita with Linus. Benita had called Nikki and they had talked for a long time. Benita was fine and promised to call Joshua. She had not mentioned the pregnancy and Nikki didn't ask. She was just happy to hear from her friend and she didn't want to upset her by bringing up anything painful. They talked instead about all the changes that had come over both of their lives in the past months. Benita was happy that Joshua was still friends with Nikki and she was even more happy about Lisa's transformation. Nikki whispered to her boyfriend, "Listen Linus, you have to make sure Joshua has his phone on all day. I'm not sure when she is going to call."

"How am I supposed to do that?"

"I don't know. Figure something out."

Linus devised a plan. He would pretend to be interested in getting a new phone and ask to see Joshua's phone. Then he would make sure it was on.

But when he started talking about new phones Joshua mentioned that his phone was a dinosaur and when Linus asked to see it He reported that it was in the car because the battery was dead and didn't hold much of a charge these days.

In all the hustle and bustle of preparing for the auction Linus forgot all about Joshua's phone until they were at the church getting dressed. Joshua's phone rang and when it did he remembered his failed mission. Nikki was on the other end, "Hey baby. You making out alright back there?"

Linus wasted no time, "Baby, I forgot! I tried to trick him into letting me see the phone so I could make sure it was on but it didn't work!"

Joshua asked, "What didn't work?"

"Oh, uh..."

Nikki whispered in his ear, "Don't you say a word! What if she already tried to call and didn't get through? He'll be devastated!"

Linus smiled at Joshua, "Nothing, just a trick Nikki wanted me to play on you that didn't work."

Joshua laughed, "Ha ha Nikki! You can't trick a trickster! I'm too slick for you baby!" He walked away feeling a bit proud of not having been tricked as Linus listened to Nikki get a little frantic about whether or not she should call Benita back and find out if she had tried to call. She decided to call her and hung up with Linus after informing him, "Ooh if you messed this up I'm going to kill you!"

Linus reminded her, "Killing is definitely not Christlike or ladylike!"

Nikki shissed back at him, "Jesus will forgive me I'm sure." she hung up and called Benita who did not answer.

~   ~   ~   ~   ~   ~   ~

The evening progressed and the auction went well. Each man performed a household talent, with points awarded for multitasking. The assortment ranged from changing a baby in record time while putting on lipstick to carrying laundry while mowing the grass and holding a conversation with a two year old. Linus' talent was floor mopping and he mopped the stage and sang a hymn wearing a housecoat, a wig with rollers and a tool belt in which he held a baby bottle, a bottle of wine, a celebrity gossip magazine, a remote control and a phone, all of which he used efficiently as he mopped the floor. The crowd laughed hysterically as he poured wine into the baby bottle and drank from it before exiting the stage.

When Joshua came out to display his talent he called for a volunteer from the audience. First Lady Jones asked, "What are you going to do for us Joshua before I select a victim?"

"I'm going to give a massage while preparing a sandwich. And then I am going to continue the massage while eating the sandwich."

The crowd laughed and hands flew up to volunteer for the massage. First Lady Jones pointed into the corner of the room and stated, "You in the yellow dress, you will do fine I think."

In the back of the room Erin stood watching. She had heard about the silent auction and figured she'd bid on Joshua and catch up with him. She had been hearing lots of rumors about Lisa but her new love, Heather, would not allow her to call Lisa's or Lisa's parents and ask any questions. Erin had vowed to Heather not to go to any lengths to contact Lisa or any of her relatives. She had neglected, in her vow making, to mention close friends so she knew she was technically not transgressing her word to Heather by seeking to make contact with Joshua.

She stood and watched in amusement as Joshua

played around on stage. She did miss him now that she saw him. She also missed Lisa. She wondered what everyone thought of her for leaving Lisa while she was in the coma but she knew she would never ask. She scanned the room searching for Lisa. Something told her that Lisa was there enjoying the holiday fun. She wanted badly to see the new Lisa. She heard that she had taken on a new feminine persona and Erin was dying to see it. The Lisa she had been with for so long had only worn a dress once the entire time they were together and that was because her sister had gotten married and Lisa was in the bridal party. Even then Lisa had changed out of the dress into a pants suit for the reception right after they had taken pictures.

The crowd laughed hard as the pregnant woman made her way to the stage. Joshua was doing warm up aerobics while she took her time getting to the stage. Nikki was out in the foyer frustrated because she could not get through to Benita and said a prayer, "Lord.

Please find a way to bring them back together. I know they were meant to be and I know you can do it. I'm leaving this in your hands. I can't take this on myself." Squeezing her way back into the Sanctuary Nikki bumped into Erin but the place was so crowded neither of the women knew who they had bumped. Nikki turned around and uttered a polite "Excuse me" into the crowd and kept moving towards the wall where she and Lisa had been watching the show. The two women had not even noticed one another.

Lisa scanned the audience. She had a strange feeling she was missing something going on in the crowd. Dismissing the thought she put her hand on Niki's shoulder and said "Don't stress Nik. If she's meant to get through to him she will. I'm living proof, God works in mysterious ways." Lisa twirled in her dress like a little girl. Together she and Nikki watched and chuckled as Joshua limbered up and the pregnant woman neared the stage.

First Lady Jones caught Nikki's eye and smiled proudly. It was a fun night and they had worked a lot to pull it off. Nikki smiled back at her and she turned and nodded towards the stage. Nikki watched the pregnant woman slowly ascend the stairs. She gasped and squealed in Lisa's ear.

Lisa jumped, "What Nik? Whats wrong?"

Nikki could not say a word. Tears flowed and she smiled wider than she knew she could. Joshua slowed his jumping about and turned around. He stopped short and in a moment the crowd fell silent. He stood there staring at the woman in front of him. Her belly was perfectly round and she was more beautiful than he remembered. Benita smiled sheepishly at him and rubbed her tummy.

Erin watched with displeasure and muttered, "Yeah, whose going to hell now?" Upset at the love scene she was witnessing between Joshua and the woman who had virtually caused her to lose the best job she had ever had, Erin turned to go. On her way out she scratched her bid off of the sheet with Joshua's name and picture on it. She glanced back one more time and caught a glimpse of Nikki in the corner with her hands to her face crying. Erin noticed there was a lovely, slender, white woman with Nikki and wondered who she might be as she turned to go. She was sure something about her was familiar but she didn't waste any time trying to figure it out.

Whispers circulated through the crowd as the two people on the stage stood staring at one another. They were both shaking and neither of them moved until Bishop yelled, "Grab her, Kiss her, tell her you love her so we can get this show on the road!"

The crowd laughed and cheered as Joshua followed the instructions to a T. He held Benita so close to him he felt their child move about inside her. He stepped back and looked at Benita as if to ask "Did you feel that?"

Benita answered his unspoken question, "Of

course I felt it silly. That's our son." Joshua lifted his hands and began to thank The Lord for bringing Benita and his son to him. The he dropped down on his knees and thanked The Lord some more. Benita stood watching and smiling. She was more than relieved at his response. She had feared that he might be angry with her for not telling him about the pregnancy.

Joshua took her hand and the crowd hushed as he spoke in a shaky voice, "Oh Benita, You're beautiful."

The crowd awed and listened intently for more as Joshua went on, "I'm so sorry for what I did to you. I'm so sorry. I love you. I love you so much. Don't ever leave me again. Stay here forever. Please, stay and be my wife. Please, don't; ever leave me again."

Benita was shocked. She had expected to have to tell him that she was prepared to deal with the responsibility of parenting alone since she had alone decided to keep the baby. She was too overwhelmed to cry but there were plenty of women crying in the audience to make up for that. At last Benita spoke, "Yes. Of course I will! Oh thank God! Yes! Yes!"

The applause and cheers were deafening. Bishop Jones walked on stage beside his wife. The crowd slowly quieted as he spoke, "Well, judging from the looks of her you two don't have much time huh?"

Laughter arose from the crowd. Nikki shouted loudly, "Do it now!" To which there were several voices repeating it as a chant. In a moment the entire crowd chanted "Do it now! Do it now!"

Joshua stood up and threw his hands up asking Benita what she thought. She returned the gesture and they turned to Bishop Jones who held his wife's hand and smiled. The crowd hushed again and Joshua asked, "Can we do it now?"

Bishop Jones teased, "Looks like you already done it at least once!" First lady Jones elbowed her husband playfully as Benita blushed and Joshua stood un-ashamedly next to Benita. He took her hand and

Bishop raised his hand to quiet the laughing crowd.

"Alright then, here goes. What's your name sweetie?"

Benita almost whispered, "Benita."

"Your last name sweetie. I know your first name, what's your last name?"

Benita smiled, slightly embarrassed. Of course he knew her name. He was the one who had tracked her down after all...but he could not in the moment remember if her last name was Rogers or Roberts "Oh, Rogers sir."

"Okay, who gives this woman away to be wed?"

A voice spoke out of the crowd. It was a deep familiar voice to Benita. "I do Bishop!" Benita's parents emerged from the crowd and it was more than Benita could handle. She began crying tears of joy as her parents made their way to the stage. Joshua shook Mr. Rogers' hand firmly. Mr. Rogers pulled him close and hugged him.

Nikki searched the crowd for Linus. He stepped close behind her and wrapped his arm around her. He pulled Lisa in close too and they watched happily as Bishop Jones gave a fast rendition of the wedding vows for them to repeat. He then reminded them of the seriousness of what they were embarking on together and charged everyone in the room to help them to uphold their vows.

Nikki said slightly more loudly than she had intended "I will!"

Bishop Jones turned and asked , "What was that?" to which many members of the audience replied, "I will."

"Well then I now pronounce you Mr. and Mrs. Joshua Brown. You may now kiss your wife...again!" Joshua obeyed happily as First Lady Jones elbowed her husband again. He planted an unexpected but welcome kiss on her.

The crowd cheered and people found spouses,

friends, sons, aunties, ushers and strangers to plant kisses upon cheek and lip and hand accordingly. Linus squeezed Nikki and kissed her gently saying, "You're next."

As unofficial and informal as it was Niki could not have imagined a more perfect or romantic proposal. She smiled and kissed him again sweetly.

At the end of the night as the winning bids were announced Mrs. Jones read the winning bid for Joshua..."We have an Erin...wait... it's scratched out, I can't really read it. Erin something...with a bid of $900! Wow she really wants a massage huh? Are you in here Erin? If so raise your hand and claim your prize. He's all yours on Saturday."

Lisa and Joshua stared wide eyed for a moment at each other through the crowd. They both scanned the room as First Lady Jones announced, "Okay Erin, you got ten seconds to claim your prize or it goes to the next highest bidder." The crowd counted down from ten to zero and Joshua was given to Mother Harris for Saturday servitude.

Nikki asked Lisa, "Do you think that was your Erin"

Lisa shrugged her shoulders, "I don't have an Erin Nik. Wherever she is, she belongs to The Lord. I just pray she knows it."

The friends looked back on how much had changed since that same time last year and Lisa stated once again, "Yeah guys, I'm living proof. I say it all the time, The Lord works in mysterious ways."

Benita smiled at her with a kindness her own sin had caused her heart to know. She had prayed much for Lisa in her time away. She had prayed for all the people she had judged so severely, including herself.

Bishop Jones gave a short benediction and the crowd dispersed. The friends stayed behind with the

Women's Department to put the sanctuary back in order.

Every one of them knew their lives had just begun anew.

www.ingramcontent.com/pod-product-compliance
Lightning Source LLC
Chambersburg PA
CBHW052025020726
47501CB00004B/1251